BENNA ELSE

PROMINENT
B O O K S
EDGE

5830 E 2nd St, Ste 7000 #9983
Casper, WY 82609
USA

CONTENTS

MONICA

"**I**'m pregnant." her voice soft almost sad as she spoke into her cell phone.

"Are you serious?" he asked.

"Yes'"

"Monica, I love you and you know that."

"Yes, I know but I won't divorce my husband. He might not be the best husband but we have two children. I have to think about how a divorce would affect them."

"You know I'd be a good stepfather." he said calmly.

"I'm sure you would be. But the point is I married young and I want to make this marriage work. It's unfortunate that you and I met when I was vulnerable. If I hadn't been legally separated and began working for you, this might not have happened." Monica sighed.

"Please Monica…" his voice now filled with pain and sadness. "You are the only woman I've ever loved. I never planned on meeting anyone who made me know love."

Silence

"This child, our child that I'm carrying will be loved intensely. I love you but I made a commitment to stay with my husband. And he's stopped drinking altogether. We don't argue anymore.

He's worked hard to treat me with love and respect. I don't want to be the reason why he could fall off the wagon."

"What about me? What about my feelings? And what about my child?" His questions were filled with deep emotions.

"I'm so sorry. I didn't plan on having any more children. Especially not like this. But I promise you this, if you will be okay with it I'll stay in touch. And if you want I will send pictures. Does that seem cruel?

I don't know how else to handle a situation like this. I don't want to hurt you anymore than I'm doing right now. I don't want to hurt my husband Michael either."

"Have you told your husband about the pregnancy?"

"No, I'm trying to decide if I should have him think it's his child."

"Obviously, no matter what I say, you've made up your mind. I just want you to know if you need or want anything just contact me. And if you decide to get a divorce I'll pay all expenses."

"I'm sorry I didn't meet you ten years ago." Monica said as she choked back tears.

"I have to go now."

"Goodbye." he said before the phone went silent.

Monica placed her phone down on the kitchen table before placing both her hands on her stomach. As she looked out of the kitchen window she sighed. Yes, this child would know love and maybe the baby's father would be able to see it sometime. She'd figure something out.

LAUREN

*L*auren moved through the crowd of mourners. This was the most heart wrenching day she'd ever experienced in her 12 years of life. The death of her mother had come quickly. Lauren hated cancer and hated the way her mother had suffered. No matter the treatment, her mother, Monica couldn't seem to fight hard enough.

Lauren found her brother Anthony sitting with a relative speaking in quiet tones. Lauren loved her brother even though he was 8 years older he'd always taken time to listen to her and teacher how to play various sports. Even in his teens he'd let her hang out with his friends when she asked.

"Excuse me," Lauren said as she approached her brother. "I can't find Tamara to let her know I'm going up to my room. I'm so tired."

"I understand. I'll let Tam know where you are. This has been so hard on you. I'll have her check on you in a while." Then he reached out giving his young sister a loving hug.

Released from the hug, Lauren continued upstairs to her room. About halfway up the stairs she turned looking back at the sea of people who knew and loved her mother. Most of the mourners were family and neighbors. However, there were some she had never met. All were sympathetic and said kind words but that did not stop the pain Lauren felt in her chest.

Once in her room Lauren fell onto the bed. The room was dark with the only sources of light coming from the hallway and a small night light on the other side of her room. Lauren had purposely kept her window drapes closed after her mother's death.

"Lauren, are you awake?" she heard a man's voice. Lauren had not realized that she'd fallen asleep. Turning from laying on her side onto her back Lauren slowly opened her eyes. With light from the hallway, Lauren saw the silhouette of a man standing just inside the doorway.

"Yes, kind of," she said after she yawned.

"I'm a friend of your mother. I wanted to tell you personally just how very sorry I am. Your pain must be great."

"Who are you?" Lauren asked as she sat upright.

"Oh, you won't remember me. I've known you since you were born. But I moved from here about 5 years ago. I have something to give you. It's something your mother and father wanted you to have. Would you always wear it?"

"Really? Why yes!"

The man walked toward her, extended his hand that held a silver necklace with a teddy bear pendant. Lauren noticed he had slender fingers with a gold band on his little finger. And he was white.

"If you ever need anything please have Michael contact me." his voice was filled with sadness.

Before Lauren could reach and turn on her bedside lamp he had walked away, disappearing into the hallway. After turning on the light, she inspected the cute pendant.

The back of the pendant read "U R Loved Mom & Dad"

Lauren fell back to sleep holding the necklace in her hand.

LAUREN 13 YEARS LATER

*E*xiting the revolving doors, Lauren walked through the gray marbled floor lobby to the security desk. Behind the desk sat two gray-haired men in security uniforms.

"Good morning gentleman," Lauren said.

"Good morning," came the response from one of the men. The other continued watching the monitors at the desk. "How can I help you?"

"My name is Lauren Boyd and I'm a new employee at the law office of Allan Hess. Mr. Hess also gave me a key so I can get into the office. I have my badge but I was instructed to stop here first." Lauren said as she handed her identification badge to the guard.

He took it from her hand, scanned it and then smiled as he handed it back. "Welcome Ms. Boyd, you're quite early. Most of the offices in the building don't open until after eight. And at this time we only have one elevator that's in service."

"Yes, Mr. Hess told me but he said he was okay with me coming in at 7:30 since I'm working part-time."

With a smile of approval from the guard, Lauren walked through the electronic gate heading for the elevator. There was only one elevator with its doors open. When she stepped in, she was surprised that it was occupied. A tall man with smooth chocolate skin was standing in the back corner of the elevator. He was reading his tablet.

"Good morning." Lauren said in her cheerful voice.

He nodded his head slightly, acknowledging her greeting but said nothing and returned to his reading.

How rude Lauren thought as she pressed the button for the 19th floor. She noted that the 20th floor was already lit. This office building was just twenty stories with the top floor being the corporate offices of Landau & Associates. This corporation was based here but had ties worldwide. Lauren thought that the man occupying the elevator was probably an executive of that company.

The doors of the elevator closed and began its ascent. It wasn't long before it began to slow down. When it came to a stop and the doors opened, Lauren turned quickly to the man and said, "Make your day great." The man looked surprised as Lauren walked away without looking back.

Lauren entered the reception area. There were several smaller offices beyond the reception desk. Mr. Hess' office occupied the very back of the area. Adjacent to his office was the conference room. Mr. Hess' secretary, Ella, had her desk to the right of his door. The desk that Lauren would occupy was across from Ella's.

Ella had emailed Lauren regarding her first day duties. Lauren got busy alphabetizing the files on her desk, then taking and filing them in the file room. By the time she completed that task, Ella had arrived.

"Good morning, Miss Gilmore," Lauren said as she watched Ella Gilmore place her purse in her bottom desk drawer.

"Good morning yourself. And please call me Ella. We're pretty informal. So I see you've completed the filing. I remembered you said you'd come to work early but I had no idea you'd get so much done. Thanks."

"I like coming early. No distractions." Lauren replied.

"Okay, once Mr. Hess gets in, we'll see what else he wants you to work on."

At exactly 8:30 Allan Hess strolled in. He was tall and lean with thinning light brown hair. His eyes were so blue they looked azure. He looked to be in his mid to late 40's but he moved like an athlete.

"Morning Ella, Lauren. Ella give me 10 minutes then come into my office. We've got a busy day." Then he went into his office, closing the door behind him.

The rest of the morning Ella, Mr. Hess and three other attorneys were in conference. Lauren answered the phone and scheduled appointments for Mr. Hess. By 10:35 Ella and the three attorneys emerged from Mr. Hess' office.

"Okay, Lauren, you need to come with me. We are going to the courthouse. Mr. Hess wants me to show you around."

Lauren only worked part time three days a week at the law office. She had a second job working at a fitness center named 2B Fit. A former two story storefront building now housed a modern workout facility. Treadmills, stationary bikes, elliptical and various weight machines occupied the main floor. Free weights and serious weight equipment were toward the rear of the main floor. On the second floor of the building were aerobics classrooms, locker rooms, showers, and restrooms.

Lauren would have thought by now she would have figured out what she wanted to do with her life. But no. After her mother's death Lauren had gone into a deep depression. Her father offered little comfort. And her brother and sister had returned to their own lives.

Her brother Anthony rarely came home even during school breaks. He'd rather be with his college friends. And her sister, Tamara worked as a nurse in another city that was over 200 miles away. Throughout her high school years, Lauren felt like a loner. After high school graduation she got a job at a retail store. Fortunately, those co-workers were nice and helped her come out of her shell. Especially one named Jeanette.

Jeanette was a hard worker and a goal setter. She wanted to become a nurse. She saved all the money she could by working two jobs. Not only did she work at the retail store five days a week but she also worked weekends at a convenience store.

It was Jeanette's drive that encouraged Lauren to deal with her depression and be forward thinking. Now they were roommates. Jeanette was now a nurse at Northwestern Hospital. Lauren had continued living at home with Michael, her father until he told her she needed to move out.

It was fortunate that Jeanette had a two bedroom apartment. Lauren thought that she would finish college before moving out on her own. Since all the memories that she'd experienced were tied to that house.

Then one day out of nowhere Michael gave notice.

"I'm giving you 2 weeks to get out." Michael's words were slurred. He'd been drinking again.

"What do you mean move out? This is my home!"

Lauren said. His words had come as a complete surprise.

"No, it's my home. The only reason I've let you stay this long is because of a promise I made to your mother. You wasted two years by not going to college right after high school. In my book your time in this house is kaput. Two weeks!" Then he turned his back swaying as he walked back to his recliner.

Lauren was stunned. She attempted to plead her case with her father but to no avail. Running upstairs to her room with tears streaming down her cheeks, she phoned her best friend.

Jeanette to the rescue. "You're coming to live with me. Haven't we planned that all along? We were just waiting until you graduated law school, right?"

That move had taken place 4 months ago. Now it was June and Lauren would graduate law school soon.

THE ELEVATOR

On Tuesday and Wednesday the scenario was repeated. Lauren would get onto the elevator and the same man would be there in the same spot. She'd speak and he'd nod but not say a word. Lauren wondered if he had mental issues. But she quickly dismissed that idea. He's probably one of those uptight executives who feels that he doesn't have to speak to someone like me, Lauren thought.

However, each day when she exited the elevator she wished him well.

The following Monday it rained causing Lauren to be a couple minutes behind schedule. Her rubber boots squeaked as she trotted toward the closing elevator doors.

"Hold the doors, please!" she called out.

A hand shot out, stopping the doors from closing. It was his hand.

"Thanks." Lauren said as she stepped into the elevator. With a tote bag, purse, and umbrella, she was attempting to push the button to her floor.

"I'll get it." he said as he pressed 19.

"Thanks again."

"Do you come to work later on Thursday and Friday?"

"No, I just work 3 days here."

"Oh." Was all he said before returning to his spot in the elevator. But he didn't begin reading; he was looking at her. "The way you're dressed you remind me of Paddington."

As the elevator doors closed. Lauren turned to look at him. "Yes, I guess I do. But I enjoy walking in the rain." Lauren said as she removed her red rain hat and shook her head from side to side releasing her curly dark hair. "And I don't have a blue coat but I have yellow boots."

"Yes you do." he smiled.

The elevator stopped and the doors opened.

"You make."

Before she finished the sentence he said, "…your day wonderful. And you as well."

The next day, Tuesday he spoke when she got on the elevator.

"Are you working with Allan Hess?"

"Yes, how do you know him?"

"I know Allan. He's an excellent attorney."

"Oh?"

"He does all of the legal work for Landau & Associates."

"Well, he was one of my law professors. That's how I happen to be working here. Myself and another student of his are working this summer."

The elevator doors closed and began its upward journey. Lauren wanted to say something more but didn't know how to continue their conversation.

"Since it seems that we're going to be riding in this elevator 3 mornings a week, we should at least know each other's name. My friends and acquaintances call me J.P." His smile was friendly. He had an accent that sounded British.

"I'm Lauren."

Their morning conveyor slowed as it got to the 19th floor. As the doors opened, Lauren stepped off and with a smile said. "You will have a great day." She heard him chuckle as the doors closed.

That evening while eating Chinese food Lauren told her roommate about J.P.

"You remember the guy I told you about who is on the elevator with me each morning." Lauren said before taking a bite of her chop suey.

"I remember you saying he was average looking, tall and chocolate. Oh and also he had an accent." Jeanette responded before sipping her tea.

"Well, today he told me his name. I'm beginning to think he's getting, I don't know, maybe comfortable with me in the elevator."

"Is that good or bad?" Jeanette asked.

"Jeanette, you've known me for a long time. I don't talk to men very much. But I'm beginning to feel a little more at ease with J.P."

"You didn't answer my question. Is it good or bad? Or maybe it's too soon to know. Afterall you just see him for about a minute 3 mornings a week. That's nothing to base a future friendship on."

"You're right but I think I'd like to go for the good if possible."

"You just have to be careful. There are some crazies out there who seem normal, then your emotions get involved. The next thing you know you're miserable, maybe even pregnant and he vanishes." Jeanette's words seemed to come from a place deep inside her soul.

Lauren looked surprised as she listened. As long as they'd known each other, Lauren knew Jeanette remained private about her teenage years.

"Jeanette don't worry. I'll be careful. He's obviously successful so why would he want to be with someone like me?"

"I wish you'd stop dogging yourself. You're not model gorgeous but who really is? You are smart, pretty and fun to be with. Isn't that what matters?" Jeannette said as she pointed her chopsticks in Lauren's direction.

"Yes, I know but for me it's hard to shake the negative words out of my head."

"Oh, you mean when you asked your father if he thought you were pretty? Jeanette said in a sour tone.

Lauren nodded. She was 15 and had needed some positive words from her father.

"All fathers should realize they are the first men in their daughter's lives. If he doesn't think she's pretty, then he's messing with her self esteem. But for him to say 'you've got a great personality and to work on that' was harsh. I bet he was drunk, wasn't he?"

"Yes, but after Mom died he pretty much stayed that way. Jeanette, let's change the subject," Lauren said. She was feeling uncomfortable.

So changing the subject meant Jeanette talked about the doctors who thought they were like gods. How some of them treated staff without respect.

"But they all aren't like that." Lauren said.

"You're right. I just need to focus on the nice ones. But sometimes they get on my last nerve." Jeanette said before digging into her lo mein noodles.

As the friends continued eating they discussed making plans for the weekend.

They both would be off this coming Sunday.

The following morning as Lauren walked toward the elevator she was aware of footsteps behind that were quickly catching up to her.

"Good morning," he said.

Lauren looked over her shoulder. It was J.P.

"Aren't you a little late?" she asked.

"Yes and I hate being off schedule."

"But it's only a few minutes. You're just usually on the elevator when I get there." Lauren said.

"Yes, that's right but I have a few idiosyncrasies. Punctuality is one of them." He said with a smile.

As they entered the elevator Lauren giggled quietly.

"I know it's kind of funny." J.P. said looking a little embarrassed.

"It isn't that. I'm just remembering your expression the first couple of days I got on the elevator."

"Was I that obvious?"

"No, I just thought you were odd. Now you make sense." She then pushed the buttons to their floors.

"Lauren, would you go to lunch with me sometime?"

Lauren's insides tightened because she was hoping to get to know this man better.

But she didn't want to seem too eager.

"I work another job on Thursday and Friday from 10 to 6:30. But maybe the first of next week would be good." she said, trying to sound calm.

"That works. I'll call you after I check my calendar."

The elevator doors opened. "I need to give you my number." Lauren said as she held the doors back.

"Don't worry, I'll call Allan's office and we can talk then. Have a great day."

After stepping off of the elevator, Lauren stood mesmerized looking at the closed doors. She grinned as she turned and walked to Allan's office area. *He asked me out, Lauren thought but he seems to be so worldly. And I've never been anywhere, wait cool your jets Lauren* thought. *He just wants lunch, not dinner or an evening on the town.*

Lauren sat down at her desk and focused on the task at hand. *A successful executive definitely would not want to be with a girl like me.*

LUNCH

Monday was the day set for lunch. J.P. had phoned as he said with Monday being his only day free at 1:00. Lauren took special care with her attire that day. So her shoulder length ringlet hair which she usually wore loose, was now pulled up into a ponytail. She decided to wear a white A-line sleeveless midi length dress with side pockets. The shoes would be a low wedge peep-toe neutral color. Minimal make-up, mascara a necessity and lip gloss.

"Well, well don't you look nice." J.P. said when she entered the elevator "There's this guy that I met. He asked me to lunch." Lauren replied.

"Do I happen to know this guy?" J.P. said, trying not to laugh.

"He works somewhere in this building. I think he's some kind of executive for Landau & Associates. You may know him." Lauren, trying her best to look serious.

"Describe him if you don't mind," J.P. said as he reached to push the buttons for their respective floors.

"H-mmm, he's a little above average in height, brown skin, close cropped hair, and nicely trimmed beard. He seemed so serious I felt sorry for him so I agreed to have lunch." Then they both laughed.

"So is this a pity lunch?" J.P. asked.

"If he lets me pay it won't be." Lauren said as the elevator slowed to a stop.

J.P. covered his mouth with his hand to hide the surprise look on his face. Of all the first dates he'd been on, no woman had paid for a meal.

Lauren stepped off, said her usual cheery farewell remark and walked away. J.P. stood speechless as the door closed.

Lauren arrived a few minutes early at the restaurant called the Bistro & Such. She wanted to get a particular table by the window. These tables were tall with high seats that had arm rest and comfortable backs. At exactly 1:00 he walked in, glanced around and strolled toward her.

He wasn't wearing his suit jacket, instead his shirt sleeves were rolled up to just below his elbows and his tie hung loosely from his neck.

"Hi, do I look less serious?" he asked as he took a seat.

"Oh, yes. This is a good look for you." Lauren said.

The waitress came over to ask for their drink order. With a quick glance at the menu they both ordered raspberry lemonade.

"So tell me about yourself Ms. Boyd." J.P. asked after putting the menu aside.

"That would take too long. But I will tell you I'm the youngest of three. I have a brother who lives in Georgia and my sister lives down state in Bloomington, Illinois. My mother died when I was 12 and my Dad's a drunkard."

J.P. was stunned with her blunt revelation. He was speechless.

"I...I don't know what to say. You seem so happy and carefree."

"It's okay, I mourned the loss of my mother for a long time. It was hard but my friends, especially Jeanette, helped. My mother poured love on me all the time she was here. I have those memories and that's what I think about each morning." Lauren sighed and then smiled. "Now, it's your turn."

"I'm the oldest of three. I have two sisters who are married and live out of state. My folks live in Peoria, Illinois. My father was injured on his job when I was in my first year of college. I worked full time during the summer months and part-time while carrying full credits during the school year. My middle sister worked after school, my mother worked as a waitress, and my youngest cared for Dad until he was able to get around." J.P. stopped talking and resting his chin in his hand with his elbow on the chair's armrest, he stared out of the window lost in thought.

The waitress came to refill their drinks and take their food order. Lauren ordered a small salad with half a sandwich. J.P. ordered cornbeef on rye and a side of sauerkraut.

"We both seem to have had interesting childhoods." Lauren said.

"Yep, but we survived. So are you still living at home with your father?"

"No, about 4 months ago he told me I had to move. That he was selling the house and moving to New Mexico. I was upset and angry but again friends helped. Even Mr. Hess pitched in, which is how I got this summer job."

"Wow, that's harsh. But you seem to have recovered well." J.P. said.

"What choice did I have? My mother shared many life lessons with me, especially after her diagnosis. She told me that life will be filled with tears and pain. And how I handle these things will determine my success or failure. To always know that I am loved and that love will come from unexpected places. So I focus on those words." Lauren said.

They got their food then and began eating. Their conversation continued as they became more acquainted. After about 40 minutes, J.P. glanced at his watch.

"I've got to go. I have a meeting in a few minutes." he said as he began to reach into his pocket.

"Oh no you don't! My treat, remember?"

"Oh, yeah I forgot. By the way, are you working Sunday?"

"I have plans with my roommate for brunch and then shopping. Why?"

J.P. was standing now getting ready to rush away, "Would I be imposing if I invite myself to join you? I think I'd like to see you again other than on the elevator."

"Okay, we'll be at the Lincoln Hotel restaurant at 11:00."

Lauren watched him as he walked away but he surprised her. As he walked away, he turned and winked. Lauren blushed.

J.P.

As J.P. strolled back to his office he focused on the meeting. And yet, Lauren continued staying in the forefront of his mind. He enjoyed being in the company of women, especially beautiful women. So why was Lauren someone that peaked his interest? She was cute or maybe pretty but not beautiful. She did not fit the females he was usually attracted to.

He liked tall, slender women with flawless complexions and who would compliment his good looks. Lauren was slender but just a little above average in height. She had some freckles across the bridge of her nose and she had a small gap between her upper teeth. And yet her smile was sincere and endearing.

J.P. knew without conceit that he was handsome. He'd been told that most of his life. And if his parents had not drilled into his mind that looks fade and it is the inner person that makes someone handsome, he would be intolerable.

He stayed out of the limelight and focused on his career. He worked hard not allowing for any distractions. He wanted wealth and was willing to attain that goal. Except for dating someone for a period of three to six months he never committed to any serious relationships. Just P.P.F., pleasures, presents and fun. Nothing serious until he was forty and he had 5 years to go.

The afternoon meeting went well. The contracts were signed and now Landau & Associates was gaining prominence in the industrial supply world. Now at home, J.P. stood looking out of the living room window with a view of Lake Michigan. His dwelling was a 20 story condo in the only high rise building that was east of Lake Shore Drive.

The city of Chicago had an ordinance that no building could be built east of Lake Shore Drive but somehow this exclusive high rise residence was built. J.P. loved his home but he found it to be too quiet lately. It seemed that ever since Lauren had entered his life, everything seemed quiet.

Those 3 mornings a week brought him pleasure. She was like a ray of sunshine in his normal routine. He admitted to himself that the first week on the elevator he felt annoyed. Now, he liked noise, her noise. Her voice, her style of dress and especially her hair. It wasn't wavey or kinky. The only term he could put to it was "curl-linky" and he liked it.

What's going on with me, he thought as he turned away from the window. *I need to go out with someone*. Reaching for his phone he called Rowena.

SUNDAY

On Monday through Wednesday Lauren worked her second job from 3:30–6:30. On Thursday through Saturday she worked from 10:00–6:30. She also taught an intense stretch class for 45 minutes on Tuesday, Thursday at 5:30 and Saturday mornings at 9:00.

Lauren arrived at her second job at 3:30. Chris, her co-worker, was busy speaking with a club member. Lauren went into the back office area to clock-in. She would work with Chris at the reception desk until 15 minutes before she taught her flexibility & stretch class.

Sitting down at her computer monitor she greeted Chris.

"Has it been busy today?" Lauren asked.

"Not too busy. I started my shift at noon." Chris said.

Before they could have any conversation a group of five people entered. They wanted information about membership. Chris began explaining while Lauren called Derek, the owner to the front.

Derek emerged from his office looking as always the perfect specimen of a physically fit man. Tall, blonde, gray eyes, and muscular shoulders. The tee shirt he wore was tight enough to show off his defined abs.

After introducing himself, Derek ushered the group into a small office where he could explain the various memberships. He had Chris follow with membership applications, pricing information and a laptop.

Lauren knew that Derek would have those people signed up for an annual membership within the hour. So Lauren allowed herself to mentally review her lunch date. *J.P. is so handsome,* Lauren thought. *And that wink, what did that mean? Then asking if he could join Jeanette and her for lunch. What was he up to?* Lauren was anxious to tell her roommate everything.

The group of five left with new membership access cards. Derek returned to his office rubbing his hands together and smiling. He had added to the growth of his business.

Chris returned to his seat next to Lauren shaking his head.

"It amazes me how Derek talks people into signing up for membership. He doesn't give all the options unless the people have done their homework ahead of time.

He has an excellent facility so why he doesn't explain everything in detail?" Chris said.

"Greed." Lauren said.

"Yes, I suppose you're right. Let's change the subject. How's Jeanette doing?"

"Good, just working too many hours. You know there's a shortage of nurses."

"Yes, but the few times we've gone out I think she had a good time." Chris said.

"You're right."

"So I've been calling and texting and haven't gotten a response. Did I do something wrong?"

"Not you, I think she has a hang-up with the fact you're 5 years younger. And you know she wants the man in her life to earn much more money than she earns." Lauren spoke quietly in sympathetic tones.

"Well, I can't do anything about my age but once I graduate in December with my degree in cybersecurity, my salary will be substantial." Chris said.

"I'll not ask what that amount means but I hope it's more than $70K a year."

"It is."

"Tell you what. Why not join us for Sunday brunch." Lauren suggested.

"Really? Great, what time and where?"

Lauren told him all the information. And she also told him that she would put in a good word with Jeanette.

Before leaving 2B Fit, Derek asked Lauren into his office.

"Lauren, how do you like working here?" Derek asked as he leaned forward resting his forearms on the edge of his desk.

"It's fun. The clients are nice and Chris and I have a good working relationship. Why are you asking?"

"I've decided to create a new front desk position. And I thought you'd be a good fit. Now before you say no just listen. You'd be the front desk coordinator. You'd make sure that all shifts for the front desk were covered and if someone couldn't make their shift, you'd find someone to cover it or maybe you might have to do it."

"Would there be an increase in salary?"

"Of course." Derek smiled now leaning back in his chair.

Lauren was surprised as she looked at the confident expression on Derek's face. She could always use some extra money. "Derek, I'll have to think about this. You understand I will be done with school by December."

"Yes, but I hope by then there will be someone who will take your place. I just need someone right now. I'm expanding, opening another facility in Schomberg. If I know this place is covered then I won't have to worry."

That evening after work, Lauren walked the 2 miles home. Her thoughts were on her friend, Chris and this new possible position at the health club. Lauren knew that Derek had made moves on some of the other female employees and she didn't want to be in his line of fire. But again the extra $10.00 an hour wouldn't hurt.

Then her thoughts shifted to Chris. He was adorable in a very studious way. Tall and angular with dark wavy hair he looked exactly the opposite of a man Jeanette would date. Jeanette was above average in height. Her hair was in long braids which complimented her honey brown skin.

Jeanette has been specific about the men in her life. Older, mature and wealthy. However, there was a secret in her youth that she would not talk about. To Lauren, whatever Jeanette's past event was, it was too painful and buried very deep in Jeanette's soul. So when she met Chris on a visit to 2B Fit they seemed to hit it off. They exchanged contact information and went out several times. Then for some reason Jeanette began avoiding Chris. I'll just have to see what happens Sunday, Lauren thought just as she entered her apartment building.

By 10:30 Sunday morning, Lauren was urging Jeanette to leave. She wanted to get to the restaurant early enough so they would beat the brunch crowd.

With Lauren's sharing how Chris had deeper feelings and wanted a more serious relationship, Jeanette acquiesced.

"Okay, I'll be nice to Chris. And it isn't that I don't care for him, it's just me. I have issues, bad memories and I don't want to hurt him." Jeanette had said when Lauren told her about Sunday brunch. Lauren didn't mention his potential salary. She just hoped Jeanette would allow her feelings for Chris to grow naturally and not be so concerned about the age difference or her past.

The two women arrived at 10:45 and they got the last available booth. A few minutes before 11:00 Chris walked in and saw them immediately. Wearing a baseball cap, a green shirt which made his hazel eyes stand out, and khaki shorts he looked very nice.

After greetings he sat next to Jeanette.

"Are we waiting for someone else?' Chris asked.

"Yep. Lauren's elevator man." Jeanette teased.

"Oh, so we get a chance to meet him. She mentioned him to me a couple of times in passing." Chris said as he smiled at Lauren.

Lauren checked the time on her phone. It was 2 minutes before the hour.

"He'll be here." Lauren said.

At exactly 11:00 J.P. strolled into the restaurant looking handsome and confident.

He wore a teal blue shirt, dark gray slacks and a smile as he headed toward their booth.

As he walked in a number of women watched him but he was oblivious to their stares. "Good morning. How's everyone?" he said after sitting down next to Lauren.

Lauren made the introductions. He shook hands with Chris and Jeanette. The waiter came over before anyone could say anything to introduce himself and explain the menu options.

J.P. suggested they start with mimosas which was agreeable to all. The women decided to split a Belgian waffle with sides of ham steak and sausage links. Chris ordered a cheese omelet and bacon on the side. J.P. ordered a short stack of pancakes with fresh fruit on the side.

Breakfast conversation flowed freely with J.P. asking both Chris and Jeanette about their jobs. He seemed genuinely interested in what each one said. After hearing Chris' goal, J P. said, "Tell you what, give me your number." I'll speak to some people and when you graduate, I'll see to it that you have a job. Landau is an international company and they need honest, eager professionals like you."

Chris was elated with the possibility of a job with Landau & Associates. He eagerly gave J.P. the necessary information. About that time the waiter asked if separate checks were needed.

"No, I've got it." J.P. said.

"J.P. we can give you our share of the check." Lauren offered.

"Nope." he said as he stood up reaching into his pocket to retrieve his wallet.

"Let's go." As he dropped two $50's on the table.

Lauren was dumbstruck. She figured J.P. was a highly paid executive but she was surprised by this gesture.

"What's next?" J.P. asked.

The group of four were standing outside by now. A sunny Sunday with mild temperatures and a warm breeze coming off Lake Michigan. Lauren and Jeanette wanted to shop at a resale shop that was located on north Wells Street. So they began walking south with Chris and Jeanette going ahead of Lauren and J.P.

"J.P that was so very nice of you to pay for our meals. You know you really didn't need to do that." Lauren said.

"Yes, I know," he said as he continued looking straight ahead.

Lauren was at a loss for words. She wanted to say something witty or clever but nothing was coming to mind.

"Is Jeanette dating Chris? She's very lovely." J.P. said.

"Well, they've dated but it's hard to say."

"What do you mean?"

"I don't want to be a gossip but Chris wants to have a more serious relationship. I didn't know if Jeanette is ready for that yet. Why are you asking?" Lauren asked.

"Just curious." he said as he looked in Lauren's eyes.

Lauren smiled before averting her gaze toward her friends. Was J.P. thinking of getting close to Jeanette? He was a man who could have just about any woman. Would he go after her best friend?

When they reached the resale shop the guys decided to go to a nearby custom bicycle shop in the next block. They agreed to meet in an hour at a spice shop that was across the street from where they were.

"That's one good looking man." Jeanette said as they entered the shop.

"Who, J.P., I guess so." Lauren said, trying not to sound concerned.

"And you said he's never been married. That's hard to believe. But then again a man who looks like that couldn't really be trusted to be faithful, right?" Jeanette said as she started looking at the blouses on the rack.

With a furrowed brow, Lauren began looking through the dress racks. But her joy of shopping had waned. Would Jeanette attempt to begin a relationship with J.P.? How would it affect her? Lauren's mind was in a spin. Afterall, what was her relationship with this man who just happened to ride an elevator 3 days a week. Am I desperate? I know that he's too good for me. Like Jeanette warned "be careful he could be a love 'em and leave 'em kind of guy." She had said those words when Lauren had told her about their lunch date.

Lauren decided that she would protect her roommate from J.P. It was Chris who deserved Jeanette if anyone did. I'll talk to J.P. on Monday. With a sigh and resolve Lauren focused on the task at hand, shopping for bargains.

An hour later, they met in the spice store. Chris was pumped after watching J.P. purchase a custom bike. He walked toward Jeanette who was trying to decide which paprika to purchase. He had to tell her the price of a bike which blew his mind. Speaking in low tones Chris shared the amount J.P. paid. "Are you kidding me?" Jeanett said. Chris nodded.

J.P. had joined Lauren who was test-tasting different cooking oils.

"Find anything you like?" he asked.

"Yes, I think so. We're running low on sunflower oil and avocado oil. What about you? Did you find a bike you just couldn't live without?"

"You could say that. Listen, I've got to go. Thanks for allowing me to be with you and your friends. I'll see you in the morning." Then he turned and waved at Chris and Jeanette before leaving the store.

As soon as he was gone, both Jeanette and Chris made a bee-line to Lauren. "Chris just told me that J.P. paid over $3,000 for a bike!" Jeanette's tone was filled with amazement.

"Yeah, he just pulled out his credit and it was a done deal." Chris said. Then he added, "Someday I'll have that kind of money."

After a bit more shopping, the three friends began walking home. Walking halfway, Chris separated from the women to go toward his home. Before he left, he pulled Jeanette aside to kiss her.

"That was sweet that you let Chris kiss you." Lauren said.

"Yeah, well it isn't that I don't like him. I just want a man that's established and with deep pockets. Speaking of which, who is J.P. and what exactly does he do?"

"I really don't know that much about him. I assume he's an executive with Landau & Associates. I get the feeling he works as a consultant."

"Well, he's the kind of man I'd like to get to know better."

"Now wait a minute. Didn't you warn me about men like him?" Lauren asked.

"Yes, but that's because you really haven't had any experience with men. You even told me when we first became friends that you never dated. J.P. strikes me as a man who knows his way with women." Jeanette said with a smile.

"Even so, I don't think you're his type." Lauren said, sounding defensive.

"And I suppose you are? Jeanette then paused, and put her hand on Lauren's shoulder. "Look, we had a good day today. I don't want us to argue. I just feel that you would be good with Chris."

"And you and J.P. are better suited." Lauren said, finishing her roommate's sentence.

"Well, I'd like to get to know him. And aren't you two just friends?" Jeanette asked with a sly smile.

"I guess so." Lauren began to have an uneasy feeling in her gut.

"So, just feel him out for me. You know, ask him what he thought of me, stuff like that." Jeanette placed a friendly arm around Lauren's shoulders.

"I'll think about it." Lauren said in a quiet voice.

That night as she lay in bed, Lauren began to question what her relationship with J.P. really was. Is he just stringing me along And if so for what purpose? He's quite good looking so why would he want to be with someone like me? Or maybe that's why.

When he's with someone who is average looking, he gets all of the attention which may be what he wants. No, he isn't like that. She wouldn't allow herself to think of him that way.

Just before drifting off to sleep, she decided to talk to him about Jeanette. After all, it may help her better understand his feelings.

AND SO IT BEGINS

"**G**ood morning Lauren. You look lovely on this Monday morning."

"Thanks J.P. and you're no slouch yourself." Lauren said as she punched the numbers for their floors.

"Well, thanks," he said with a chuckle.

"J.P. what did you think about my friend Jeanette?"

"What do you mean?" he asked as he arched one eyebrow.

The elevator doors closed and their conveyance began to ascend.

"She was asking me about you and me. I think she'd like to get to know you better." Lauren maintained a poker face although her insides were in turmoil.

"She's very pretty but I've only met her once. So it's hard to judge anyone. Are you trying to play matchmaker?"

"I'm not doing that but I think you two…I just think you'd look great together."

The elevator stopped, the doors opened and Lauren bolted out. But J.P. ran after her, grabbed her by the arm and turned her around. He saw tears in her eyes.

"Lauren, don't do this." J.P. said before hugging her.

"It's allergies." she said, wiping her eyes with the back of her hand. She pushed herself out of his hug.

"Look, you and I have a good relationship. Why can't we keep it that way?

And as far as Jeanette goes, she's really not my type." J.P. said.

"She isn't?" Lauren said in a surprised voice.

"No."

"But she's intelligent and beautiful."

"There's more to relationships. Believe me I know. Now look, I've got to go. But we can talk more Wednesday at lunch, okay?" J.P. said.

"Oh, okay. Can I call you later?"

"Yes, of course." J.P. said. Then just before walking away he said, "Make your day wonderful."

Lauren smiled and waved.

On Wednesday, Lauren and J.P. were having lunch along the banks of the Chicago River. Lauren had packed a picnic lunch for them. Oven fried chicken, homemade potato salad, chips, chocolate cookies for dessert. And she brought a choice of beverages either alcohol free beer or ginger beer.

"Did you cook all of this?" J.P. said before taking another bite of the chicken thigh.

"Yes, except for the chips." Lauren beamed.

"Are the spices in this from that spice store?" J.P. asked.

Lauren nodded as she sipped her beverage. It was a beautiful summer day. The summer blue skies in Chicago seem bluer because of Lake Michigan. No clouds today, just warm sun and a gentle breeze.

Lauren, wore a pale pink sleeveless dress with her curly hair held in place with a white and pink bandana. Pink hoop earrings, pink, gold and white bracelets graced each wrist.

"Did I tell you how nice you look today?" J.P said with a smile.

"No, but that's okay." Lauren said.

"No it's not okay. Friends should compliment each other. And with your dark hair and your natural tan skin you look perfect. May I please ask, what's your ancestry?" J.P. asked.

"I just know that my father is white but my mother didn't know her parentage. She was found abandoned without any information. She was adopted by an African-American couple who had three boys and wanted a girl." Lauren explained.

"So do your mom's parents live in Chicago?"

"No, they moved after Mom died. They didn't like my father and blamed him for my mother's death."

"Wow, Lauren I'm so sorry."

"It's okay. I talk to them once a week and I plan on visiting them soon. Once I'm through with school."

They were sitting on a bench with the picnic basket between them. The small ice chest was on the ground by Lauren's feet.

J.P. as usual glanced at his watch. Lauren knew he'd have to go soon. He always had a meeting to go to.

"Before I leave, are you still wanting to go biking Sunday?"

"Yes but let me get this straight. You and your buddy Glen are riding to Evanston from Navy Pier then turning around and coming back. I'm meeting you both at the North Avenue pedestrian bridge, right?" Lauren said.

"Yep, then the three of us will continue south. Glen and I are just going as far as Hyde Park then returning back to Navy Pier. I don't expect you to go that far. But do you think you could bike to Navy Pier? You could wait for us there," J.P. said.

"Yes I can do that. Sounds fun."

"Great. I'll call you when I think we'll be close enough for you to meet us." J.P. said. He then began to help pack up the left overs before leaving.

THE BIKE RIDE

"J.P. is this just another conquest?" Glen asked.

"What do you mean by another conquest?" J.P. asked before sipping his cup of coffee.

"I've known you a long time. You date, you have fun and then you break up." Glen smiled.

"Are you keeping tabs?" J.P. asked.

"Jackie and I are concerned. How many hearts are you going to break?"

"I don't break hearts. I just get tired or maybe even bored. It seems the women I date are not fun. I need spontaneity and laughter." J.P. said.

"So this Lauren has that?" Glen smirked.

J.P. grinned, "She makes me smile. When I have a hard day she somehow removes my stress. I can't explain it but she doesn't know everything about me. And you promised not to say anything." J.P.'s tone changed and became serious.

"I've kept that promise for years now. But you really need to stop this. It's getting old." Glen said.

"Please tell your wife not to worry. And you my dear friend, I apologize."

Glen nodded and said that they'd better get going. After paying the check the friends began their ride. Riding east on Grand avenue to the bike trail along the lake shore then turning north to go on the first leg of the ride. The waters were calm in the lake. The early morning runners, dog walkers and other riders were few. The sun was beginning to peek over the horizon. Both men's bikes were equipped with rear flashing red lights and white beams on the front. They also had reflective strips on their clothes.

It took a little over an hour going at a steady pace to reach Evanston city limits. They stopped and did a few stretches before making the return trip. As they approached Belmont avenue, J.P. phoned Lauren.

"We should be meeting you in about 15–20 minutes," he said.

"I'm already waiting, I know how punctual you are. And heaven forbid if I was late." she laughed.

"Am I that bad?"

"Yes."

"See you in a bit."

Lauren sat on a nearby bench observing the sunrise. Even though there was automobile traffic behind her, the water lapping onto the sand, people just exercising made it seem peaceful.

Lauren mentally reviewed her conversation with Jeanette before leaving to meet J.P.

"So you and J.P. are still just friends and nothing more?" Jeanette said.

She'd just come home after working a 12 hour shift.

"Yep. Just talking, eating and enjoying each other's company."

"I still find it hard to believe. There's got to be something wrong." Jeanette said as she walked into the kitchen.

"Can't a man and a woman just be friends?" Lauren asked.

"No." Jeanette said, "You be careful. He's got a plan."

Lauren watched her friend get the cranberry juice out of the refrigerator. Lauren instinctively knew that her friend was right. She also knew that she was falling in love with J.P. Lauren accepted the fact that they'd hadn't known each other very long but her feelings were strong. She was willing to accept unrequited love.

Just being with him or talking over the phone made her happy. She expected that one day he'd move on to someone else. But for now she was willing to accept whatever he was willing to give.

Changing the subject Lauren asked if Jeanette and Chris were going out.

"Yes, there's a concert in Millennial Park this evening. Chris is so sweet. He's fixing a picnic meal with all the fixings."

"So you're beginning to have deeper feelings for him?"

"Yes unfortunately. I really didn't want to but, yeah." Jeanette said with a tired smile. "I'm going to take a very warm bath and get in bed. You have fun riding." Jeanette gave Lauren a brief hug and with the juice bottle in her hand she walked into her room.

Lauren sat on a bench near the north avenue pedestrian bridge. Watching the sun slowly ascend above Lake Michigan, she thought about her life up to this point.

She recalled being very happy until she was about 8 or 9 then there was sadness. Then after that more sadness with the death of her mother. Struggling to move forward was so hard. Although her mother's words of encouragement with many hugs and kisses keep her focused on her academic goals it all seemed futile without Monica.

Then being evicted from her childhood home by the man she thought of as her father, more sadness.

But with J.P. she was happy. Though she understood that she wasn't his type of woman, she needed the emotional crumbs he tossed her way. She just hoped that someday a man would come into her life who would love her the way she felt about J.P.

The ringing of her cellphone startled her. "I see you. Get on your bike." J.P. said.

Lauren mounted her bike just as the two men pulled up next to her. The threesome headed south. Lauren kept up with them until they got to Shedd Aquarium and she began to slow down. It was apparent that she wouldn't make it even as far as McCormick Place.

"Hey, guys!" she called out.

J.P. stopped immediately when he heard her voice. He'd been watching her with the small rearview mirror he had mounted on his helmet.

"Are you ok?" J.P. asked, concerned that she'd done too much.

"You two are strong bikers and I'm not quite ready for this much riding. I'll wait here and rest. You both go onto Hyde Park. I packed a couple of things to keep me occupied. I'll join you on the return trip." Lauren said. When she and J.P. had talked about biking J.P. had suggested that she not try to make the full ride.

"Are sure you'll be alright sitting here?" Glen asked. He'd also stopped when Lauren had called out.

"Oh yeah, I'll be fine. I'll just park myself on this bench and read my book or do some sketching. I brought a small sketch pad with me. Now go on and don't worry." Lauren smiled as the men rode away.

Lauren took a long drink of water before removing her bike helmet. After leaning her bike on the back side of the bench, she sat down. After rubbing her thighs, she stood up to stretch her body, especially her legs. If biking is something J.P. enjoys, Lauren thought then she'd work on building her endurance.

As the minutes passed Lauren became engrossed in reading her book. She wasn't aware that a young woman was about to steal her bike.

"Hey you, stop!" a man shouted.

Lauren looked up quickly. The man who shouted was in pursuit of the thief. Lauren was surprised and wasn't prepared for how to act. Run after her bike leaving her items on the bench or hoping that the stranger would be able to catch the thief.

Fortunately, the stranger was fast and the young woman fell off of the bike in her attempt getaway.

"Oh my goodness. Thank you so much." Lauren said as the man approached with her bike.

"It was nothing. I just happened to be in the right place at the right time." he said.

He was a nice looking slender man of average height. His brown skin was sweaty.

It was obvious that he was a runner.

"You know you should chain up your bike," he said.

"Yes, I do know better, I just didn't imagine anyone being that bold, I mean I was sitting right there!" Lauren said, gesturing toward the bench.

"My name is Marcus and I jog here daily. I haven't seen you in this area before." he said.

"That's because I don't usually bike this way. I'm meeting some friends. My name is Lauren and thank you so much for your help."

Marcus continued holding Lauren's bike as they walked back to the bench. After chaining up her bike, they both sat down.

"Are you training for a competition or running for the joy of it?" Lauren asked.

"A little of both. I began jogging just to lose weight. It became a habit, almost an addiction. Now I'm training to do a half marathon." Marcus smiled proudly.

Just then J.P. and Glen rode up. Seeing Lauren talking to another man made J.P. feel an emotion he avoided, - discontent or maybe jealousy.

"Hey, you." J.P. said as approached seeing this man sitting next to Lauren. "Is everything alright?"

"Oh, J.P., Glen, this man saved me from losing my bike." Lauren said, startled at the sound of J.P.'s voice. She'd been facing Marcus with her back toward approaching friends.

Lauren went on to explain what had happened.

"Thanks again." Lauren said.

"No worries, you just chain your bike no matter where you are. Now I'd better get moving before I cool off too much." Then he turned and continued his run.

Glen was amused watching J.P. reacting to Lauren talking to a man that he didn't know. Usually, J.P. did not care about his other female acquaintances talking to another man. But for some reason

Lauren was having a different effect on his friend. Glen was aware of Lauren's allure when J.P. first spoke to her about weeks ago.

Today he was seeing that J.P. was totally unaware that he was having true feelings for this cute woman.

Glen's phone vibrated, it was his wife, Jackie. Speaking briefly, she told him she wanted to meet Lauren and suggested that they meet for lunch. Glen thought it was a great idea.

"Say, you two, my wife wants to meet us for lunch at her favorite pizza restaurant.

What do you say?" Glen asked.

J.P. looked at Lauren to see if she'd was agreeable to pizza for lunch, "Yes," Lauren said. This will give me more time with J.P. she thought. J.P. nodded with an added thumbs up.

The restaurant was on north Rush Street. It offered both indoor and outdoor dining. By the time the 3 bikers arrived Jackie, along with their 4 year old daughter Cassie, were seated in the patio area. After securing their bikes they join Glen's pregnant wife and child.

Glen introduced Lauren to his wife of 7 years. J.P. gave Jackie a kiss on her cheek and then he picked up Cassie giving her a bear hug causing the child to squeal with glee.

"How's my favorite 4 year old?" J.P. asked.

"Uncle J.P., I'm good." was her reply.

"I ordered already. It takes at least 30 minutes for the deep dish pizza. I hope you like the works, Lauren. I know what these two characters like." Jackie said.

"Yes, that's fine." Lauren smiled. Jackie had dark brown hair, fair complexion and green eyes. Glen was the opposite blonde hair, brown eyes, and a ruddy complexion.

And Cassie was almost a duplicate of her mother except she had hazel eyes.

Jackie asked about the ride. J.P. let Glen do the talking as he helped Cassie color with crayons in a book she brought. Lauren watched J.P. This was a side she never imagined she would see.

Water and lemonade were the drinks of choice. The pizza was enjoyed by all. It was nice and relaxed. After some time Jackie needed to excuse herself to go to the ladies room. Lauren and Cassie went along.

"J.P., Lauren is nice. You're not taking her on your boat are you?"

"Why not? I like her and we haven't spent any real time alone." J.P. smiled at the thought of Lauren.

"I know about your boat excursions. That's where your girlfriends fall in love with you. I think you're going to be surprised. I think you like her more than you realize." Glen said.

"Naw, you're wrong my friend. I'm not scheduled to fall in love for another 5 years," J.P. spoke with confidence.

Before Glen could say more, the females returned. Jackie was rubbing her pronounced stomach. "I think this baby is ready to come out. We need to get home, Glen honey,"

Immediately, he had her sit, J.P. went out to the curb to hail a cab. Jackie apologized as she leaned on her husband. J.P. picked up Cassie, while Lauren gathered Cassie's backpack putting crayons, and coloring book into it.

Glen helped Jackie into the cab. Then J.P. handed Cassie to her father who placed her next to her mother along with her backpack.

As the cab pulled away Glen unchained his bike waved to Lauren, said a few words to J.P. before departing.

"How far along is she?" Lauren asked.

"I think the baby's due in 3 weeks. But it may be sooner."

"Wow, that's nice." Lauren said

"I guess." J.P. said with a shrug of his shoulders.

"J.P. you mean to tell me you wouldn't want children?"

"Maybe someday but not at this time. There are too many other things I want.

And speaking of wanting, what are you doing next Sunday?" J.P. asked.

"No plans, why?"

The waitress approached with the check. J.P. quickly looked at the amount, produced his plastic, handing it to the young woman.

"I own a boat and I'd like to take you for a ride. Have you ever been on a cruiser out in Lake Michigan?" he asked

"No, my father was an over road truck driver, change being a mechanic working on expensive automobiles, and as he would say, 'raising a family'. We rarely went on vacations."

"Then you and I will spend the day out on the lake. You just bring a swimsuit, a pair of shoes you can wear on the deck. I'll have everything else. Oh, I've got to travel this week so I won't be with you for our usual elevator ride. I'm leaving tonight and won't be returning until Wednesday afternoon."

"Gee. I don't know if I can survive riding that elevator alone. I may just have to walk up to the 19th floor." Lauren said with a giggle.

"You're so funny." J.P. said as he hugged her around her shoulders. This was their second hug.

The waitress returned, J.P. signed the receipt. "I live south of here and you live northwest of here. Will you be okay getting home?" he asked.

"Yes. I'm not a child,"Lauren said.

"I don't want you befriending any more joggers." he said without smiling.

Lauren just waved as she got on her bike. J.P. watched her for a while before he began his ride home. He denied any feelings that he was experiencing. She was just another woman he kept telling himself.

THE BOAT TRIP-PLUS

The first 3 days of the week Lauren worked on a contract that didn't seem quite right. Unfortunately, Mr Hess was also gone. From what Ella said there was a huge negotiation taking place. The top executives plus Mr. Hess had to be in on the meetings.

They were overseas.

Early Thursday morning Lauren received a text from J.P. He was back and he would see her at her stretch class that evening. Lauren was thrilled. The fact he was back and had contacted her, the fact that he would be in her class thrilled her.

At 5:15 he hadn't shown up. He knew the class began at 5:30 so where was he? Lauren left the desk to prepare for her class. As she got her mat and greeted the students he appeared but he wasn't alone.

Lauren had to begin teaching but with each movement and every position, she would glance in J.P.'s direction. He was one of four men in the class. The rest of the students were female. The woman that had accompanied J.P. was beautiful and agile. As the class progressed, she couldn't help but notice the way that woman would look at J.P.

After class they made their way toward Lauren. "Hey, Lauren I want you to meet a friend of mine. This is Lyncoln Willis," J.P. said.

"Hello, thanks for coming to my class. I hope you enjoyed it."

"It was wonderful. You're an excellent instructor. I apologize for coming so late. It was my fault. Poor J.P. was stressing. But you probably know about his punctuality." Lyncoln said with a gorgeous smile.

"Thanks, and how do you know J.P.?"

"Oh, we met in the UK some years ago."

"You lived in the UK?" Lauren asked, looking at J.P.

"Yes, when my parents moved from the Caribbean to the UK. Then we came to the United States when I was 10." J.P. said.

"So you two have known each other since you were kids?" Lauren asked.

"Yes, best friends and we've stayed in touch over the years." Lyncoln added.

Before Lauren could say anything else, J.P. said, "Hey, come on Lyncoln we've got a date!" Then he grabbed her by the wrist rushing toward the door. They both waved before exiting.

Now Lauren was perplexed. Was their date an appointment or a date-date? Lyncoln was tall with short black hair and skin the color of ivory. Lauren hated to admit it but the two of them looked perfect together. So with this woman in town, would she be with them on the boat? Or would he break their date in order to be with her? Lauren's mind was filled with negative thoughts.

As Lauren was leaving 2BFit she saw Chris waiting in the lobby.

"Are you okay?" He asked when she got closer.

"Sure, why shouldn't I be?"

"Well, when I saw J.P. come with that beautiful brunette, I was concerned. I mean aren't you and he dating?"

"Oh, no just pals, you know, friends. That's all." Lauren hoped her attempt to sound normal would fool Chris.

"Well, If you say so." Chris said but he looked doubtful.

"No, really I'm okay, just tired. I'll see you later." Lauren said as she headed toward the back office to clock out.

All the way home Lauren considered ways to get out of her date on Sunday. She was aware that her heart was dictating her actions toward J.P. but she needed to use her head. Lauren had considered herself to be logical with a friendly, warm demeanor. Yet when she was with him, she didn't seem to be able to think at all.

Entering her apartment she heard the television. Jeanette was home.

"Hey you," Jeanette called out from the living room. "I just started watching this old classic movie. Care to join me?"

"No, not tonight. I've got a lot on my mind. I'll just take a nice shower and go to bed with a book." Lauren said as she peeked in at her roommate who was lounging on the couch.

"Well, I made chicken salad if you want some."

"I don't know, maybe later. Thanks" Lauren said as she walked to her room.

In the middle of the night, Lauren got up and went into the kitchen. All was quiet. She heard Jeanette's soft snoring which made Lauren smile. She had kidded Jeanette about her snoring which Jeanette had vehemently denied.

Opening the refrigerator, Lauren retrieved the bowl of chicken salad and a wine bottle. After preparing a small snack she took it back to her room. Thoughts of J.P. were wearing her out. She'd decided to call him and say that she'd changed her mind about Sunday. Afterall, Lyncoln was with him, probably right now.

Saturday morning Lauren's cell phone woke her up.

"Hey you! Good morning" J.P.'s cheerful voice boomed into Lauren's ear. "J.P.?"

"I just wanted to remind you that I'll pick you up at 10:00 tomorrow."

"You sound like you're outside somewhere."

"Yep, Glen and I are riding to the Illinois-Wisconsin stateline. We're just taking a brief break and I just wanted to remind you about tomorrow."

"Well, I wanted to say I don't think I can make it." Lauren said quietly. She hated herself as soon as the words came out of her mouth.

"What, why are you sick?"

"No, I just thought you and Lyncoln would want to be together."

Silence

"J.P. did you hear me?"

Then she heard him laughing. "What's so funny?" she asked.

"You,…are you serious? Me and Lyncoln wow!" he kept chuckling.

"What's so funny?"

"First of all, young lady, I don't break dates. And second as I told you she and I are long time friends but more importantly, she's married. I don't date married women no matter how beautiful."

"Oh, I just thought…" Lauren said feeling foolish.

"I can just guess what you thought. Well, don't. If I have another date or appointment, I'll be honest with you. And I expect the same from you. Is that a deal?" J.P.'s voice was firm, not angry.

Taking a deep breath Lauren said, "Yes."

"Alright then, are we good for tomorrow?"

"Yes and I'm sorry."

"Don't be. You're good for me." J.P. said.

Sunday morning, Lauren was dressed and waiting in front of her apartment building a little before 10:00. His words "you're good for me" touched her deeply. He didn't say he loved or even liked her but that was alright. The fact he appreciated her was enough. She had made up her mind that they would always be friends.

As J.P. drove to meet Lauren he wondered why he'd told her she was good for him. He'd never told any woman anything like that. He had wooed women, he'd even told some they were special but never that they were good for him.

Pulling up to her building he appreciated her outfit, not that it was anything special: an oversized shirt, shorts and canvas shoes.

Her corkscrew curls rested just below her shoulders. It was her smile, warm and sincere.

"Morning, miss, need a ride?" he said after stopping his BMW where she stood,

"Perhaps, are you the boatman who has promised to take me for a ride on his cruiser on Lake Michigan?"

"Yes, hop in."

It was a perfect day. Usually in August the humidity would be stifling but not today. Driving toward Belmont Harbor J.P. told of the bike ride with Glen. That the ride yesterday would be the last one for a while. He and Jackie were expecting the baby within the next week.

"Please give them my best. I'm so happy for them." Lauren said.

Once on the board, they motored out past the break water to the open waters of Lake Michigan. Then he opened it up heading south past McCormick Place onward as far as the Museum of Science and Industry. Then he turned the boat around to head back north. When they saw Navy Pier he stopped the boat and dropped anchor.

"Are you enjoying yourself?" he asked.

"Oh yes! This is so much fun! I was afraid I'd get sick so I did get some ginger candy but I haven't had to use it. Oh, J.P. this is great!" Lauren beamed.

"Are you ready to swim?"

"Yes." She had her swimsuit underneath her clothes so slipping out of her shorts, shoes and shirt Lauren jumped into the cool lake waters. J.P quickly removed his clothes and he was also wearing his swimming trunks under his khaki shorts. They frolicked, splashing each other, laughing and even racing around the boat.

Finally, J.P. wanted to rest so he climbed the ladder of the boat. Lauren followed and as she reached the deck J.P. offered his hand to help her on board. But he didn't let go of her hand. Instead he pulled her close and with his free hand he gently moved her wet hair from her face.

He leaned down to kiss her but Lauren placed her fingers on his lips.

"Don't do this J.P. Don't kiss me." Lauren said softly.

"Why?"

"I'm not a love 'em and leave 'em woman. If you kiss me, it would change the dynamics of our relationship. So please, let's just stay as we are. It would be safer for both of us." Lauren said as she looked into his brown eyes.

Slowly he allowed her to step away. She was right.

But why was she right, J.P. pondered as he watched her walk away and down into the cabin below deck?

J.P. climbed into the captain's chair and turned the keys to start the engines. They'd been having a great time and now because of a habit, a habit that seemed foolish now, maybe even ruined a great relationship. Glen was right. J.P. recognized that Lauren was different and he wanted to, no needed to mend this situation.

As the boat slowly motored back to the harbor, Lauren emerged from below. She was now wearing blue shorts, a blue and white tee shirt and her curls were pulled back into a ponytail.

"You look very nice." J.P. said as she came and sat opposite him.

"I try." Lauren said with a smile.

"Would you mind steering while I change?"

"I guess I can. Are you sure you can trust me?"

"Just keep straight, don't touch the throttle. I won't be very long." he said before descending into the cabin.

Lauren followed orders and found that she was enjoying this. She liked the movement of the boat as it cut through the waters. But she wondered what J.P. would do next. The expression on his face was hard to describe when she stopped him from kissing her. It seemed to be a mixture of surprise and annoyance. Thank goodness he wasn't the type to force himself on her, Lauren thought.

"How's it going?" J.P. asked as he came up behind her.

"This fun and J.P. are we still okay, I mean as friends?" Lauren asked.

"Sure…sure it was just a moment. Yeah, we're still friends."

Lauren moved out of his way so that he could take the wheel. As the cruiser picked up speed Lauren sat down at the stern. She watched him enamored with this man.

But she was determined not to give in to her feelings.

J.P. docked the boat easily into the slip. Lauren leaped out to tie the boat to the cleat. J.P. showed her the correct way to tie the stern and tie bow. After collecting their clothes J.P. locked up the cabin. Walking back to his car neither of them spoke.

It was almost two o'clock and Lauren asked to go home. She was tired.

TIME FOR A CHANGE

The summer months seemed to have flown by. Over the July 4th weekend J.P. had gone home to be with his family. He helped his father with the garden and repaired a part of the fence that was coming apart. He'd offered to pay and have a contractor do the work but Oskar wouldn't hear of it. "I taught you how to work with your hands. It is good for a man to do some physical labor. It is healthy!" J.P. didn't argue with his father.

It gave him needed time to figure out his feelings toward Lauren.

Lauren spent that time alone. Jeanette worked 2 twelve hour shifts two days prior to the holiday and on the holiday she was with Chris.

Lauren read, watched some movies and cried when she allowed herself to think about J.P. She'd never been in love. And the people who are supposed to love were out of her life for the most part. She did have her grandparents whom she phoned regularly. Her mother was dead and her father, a drunkard, had kicked her out of the only home she'd ever known. Her sister and brother had their own lives to live. Although they would stay in touch it wasn't the same.

After the holidays life returned almost to normal. Riding the elevator with J.P., having lunch on Wednesday and brunch on some Sundays or going on bike rides. J.P. shared pictures of Glen and Jackie's newest addition. The baby boy, named Gregoree, was a healthy 8.5 pounds. He had dark hair and blue eyes.

Lauren was amazed at how beautiful he was. "He's a boy so he would be handsome not beautiful." J.P. teased.

"Whatever, he's still pretty." Lauren said.

"Say, would you be willing to go on the boat again with me?"

"Yes, I'd like that. But could we do it on Saturday? I'm going to visit my grandparents Sunday." Lauren said.

Later that same day J.P. phoned. He had another idea.

"Say instead of going on my boat what do you think about horseback riding?"

"What do I think, I've never thought about it. The only horses I've seen are either in the movies or television." Lauren said.

"Are you open to trying it? I think you'd enjoy the experience."

"I don't know J.P. You've taught me how to drive, I mean steer your boat and I'm really enjoying that. But riding a horse. That kind of frightens me." Lauren said in a quiet tone.

"Honestly, I was scared when I began. However, I've been riding for over a year and loving it. And I think you'd learn to like it. You don't seem to be the type of woman who is stuck in an urban mentality. Or have I misjudged you?" J.P. said.

"Are you challenging me?" Lauren asked.

"In a way, I guess I am. Some of the women I've been with only want to attend galas, eat at fancy restaurants, have their hair and nails done and you know be alluring."

"So you're saying I'm not alluring?" Lauren teased.

Pause and quiet.

"J.P. are you still there?" Lauren asked.

J.P. didn't know how to respond. His problem, he was fighting the attraction that he felt for Lauren. Why couldn't he meet her 5 years from now? That was his timeline for a serious relationship. Not now!

"I'm here, and yes, you are alluring. So, as alluring as you are, what do you say?" Are we going horseback riding?" he said, trying to sound jovial.

"Okay, I'll do it."

The location was a west suburb of Chicago. The various buildings consisted of barns, stables, tack building as well as a corral. There was also an equestrian arena with various levels for the horse to jump.

Upon getting out of the car Lauren observed a great deal of activity. Young people in riding habits leading horses with English saddles. Others in jeans and tee shirts preparing to ride horses with a western style saddle.

"Hi, J.P." a woman called out as she approached with her hand extended in a greeting, "It's been awhile since you've been here." Her smile, warm and friendly.

"Yes it has. I've missed this." J.P. said as he shook her hand.

"And who is this?" the woman said, looking at Lauren.

"Yes, this is my friend, Lauren Boyd. Lauren, this is Alice Ludlow, manager and co-owner of this place."

"Happy to meet you." Alice said while warmly shaking Lauren's hand.

"Thanks. J.P. hasn't really told me too much about this place. But it looks very nice." Lauren said as she glanced around her surroundings.

"Not much to tell. We basically teach people to ride and feel comfortable around horses. We also board horses and do trail rides. And I believe that's what you two are doing today, right?"

"Yes and as I told you over the phone Lauren has never ridden a horse."

"Not to worry, Lauren. I've selected a very gentle mare for you to ride. And J.P., your favorite horse, Paul's Boy, is available."

"You'll be with a small group for the trail ride. So follow me, we've got some time before the ride."

They followed Alice into one of the barns. Lauren was taken aback by the smell of hay, horses and leather. As they walked, many of the stalls were empty. Alice explained there was a large group riding for 6 miles so many of their horses were on the trail. Alice also explained that the horses they boarded were kept in another building.

Finally, they stood in front of a stall where a lovely paint horse stood looking out at them.

"Lauren, this is Spot. She is very gentle. Go ahead and touch her just above her nostrils. She won't hurt you."

Lauren slowly approached the animal, extending her hand. She didn't want to appear too nervous but her knees trembled slightly. Lauren didn't want to disappoint J.P. This was something else that he enjoyed. And the fact he wanted to share this with her made it important for her to want to do it.

Spot seemed to relax which helped Lauren to also relax. It was as if Spot knew instinctively how nervous Lauren was, and she wanted Lauren to know they would be okay together.

J.P. watched Lauren as she stroked the horse. Then Alice handed Lauren some apple slices, showing her the correct way to feed a horse without losing a finger tip. J.P. was again impressed with Lauren's willing attitude to try different things. She was becoming a strong biker and she was now steering the boat without asking questions. They'd even gone fishing and Lauren had caught a fish. But when will he tell her about himself?

Of their group of 10, Lauren was the only new rider. J.P. stayed close to her riding his horse which was 16 hands tall, a beautiful Appaloosa gelding. Lauren's horse was 14 hands tall white with brown spots. On their drive to the stables J.P. had explained to Lauren that a horse's height was measured by a hand's width from ground to the highest point on their withers.

"And what are the withers?" Lauren asked.

"The horse's shoulder." J.P. said. He also explained the saddle types. What the trail was like. He truly wanted her to have a good time.

The trail was tree lined but wide enough for two horses to walk side by side. J.P. in jeans, pale green tee shirt, cowboy boots and a straw cowboy hat. He looks so handsome, Lauren had to say something.

"You look like a real cowboy. "

"Thanks but you should have seen me when I started. I over did the cowboy look. I was an urban cowboy. It was so horrible. Alice laughed so hard at me that she was in tears." J.P. admitted.

"Wow, I would have love to have seen that,"

"I'm glad you didn't." J.P. said. "By the way, you look very nice. I like your wide brim hat with the chin strap. But you seem to always know how to dress."

"I have the internet to thank. I've had this hat, but I hurried to the store after you called with a change of plans. I went to a western clothing store for my jeans. I couldn't afford the boots but if I stick with this, I'll save my pennies and get a pair." Lauren smiled at J.P.

They were half-way when the woman leading the ride halted the ride. She told all to dismount to stretch their legs. They would have 15 minutes before they would continue the ride. Each rider was to keep holding their horse's reins and just walk about. Once off their horses, J.P. took Lauren's hand as they walked slowly away from the others.

"Lauren," J.P. said as he pulled her close. "I've been wanting to do this since I saw you this morning," He gently pushed her hat back off of her head, before kissing her gently on the lips. Lauren responded in kind, wrapping her arms around his neck. J.P.'s arms encircled Lauren pressing close. His physical body seemed to be controlling his mental strength. All he had promised himself regarding love were lost at this very moment.

"Lauren, what are you doing to me?" he asked softly as he continued hugging her.

Lauren couldn't say anything. She just wanted him to keep holding her. She hoped he'd declare his love for her. She instinctively knew if she said it first, he'd back off. She didn't want to pressure him.

Slowly they stepped away from each other, Lauren smiled sweet and alluring.

While J.P. seemed a little embarrassed and yet happy.

"I'm sorry," he said.

"I'm not. It was a nice kiss. You are a good kisser. It's obvious you've done it before."

J.P. had to grin at her statement. "I've had some practice."

"How did I do?" Lauren asked.

"I need to test you again." J.P. said as he pulled her into his arms again. This time the kiss was more ardent.

J.P.'s horse began shaking his head and stomping its front hoof.

"I guess Paul's Boy is letting us know we need to get back to the trail," J.P. said, although he continued holding Lauren.

"Yes." Lauren agreed as she began to ease from their hug. Lauren put her hat back on before they both started walking back to the group. It was apparent that Alice had seen them kiss by her expression. She winked at them and seemed to give a nod of approval. Lauren smiled demurely while J.P.'s face was stoic. Again he was letting emotions dictate his actions and he didn't like it.

"Butcher!" Alice called out to the young man who'd been riding at the rear of their group. "You lead and I'll take the rear. Everyone mount up."

As they began, J.P. stayed quiet as he grappled with his emotions. Riding beside her, he'd glance at Lauren. She seemed to be more and more lovely every time he saw her.

"J.P. are you okay?" Lauren asked.

"Oh, yeah I've just got a lot on my mind." he said with a weak smile.

"I hope it's not your job. That Mr. Landau seems to take advantage of you. You get to work early and stay late many nights. Just hope he appreciates your dedication." Lauren said.

"I think he does." J.P. replied.

"Then please smile, this is your day off, right?"

J.P. smiled just as the horses began to walk faster and some started trotting. Lauren held tightly to the saddle horn and the reins. She was becoming fearful as Spot's pace quickened.

Lauren heard J.P. telling her to squeeze her legs tighter and lift her bottom slightly up off the saddle. He kept saying "You can do this. It's okay." As he spoke he reached over and grabbed Spot's reins causing the horse to slow down.

"Are you two alright?" Alice said as she came abreast to Lauren's horse.

"I...I..." Lauren couldn't seem to find words.

"We're fine. I think I'll just hold on to her reins for a bit." J.P. said. He noticed tears forming in Lauren's eyes.

"Are you sure? I can stay with you." Alice said.

"Nope, we're good." J.P. said

"Well alright but I'll be keeping an eye on you two. I don't want anything bad to happen." Alice said before turning her horse around to back to go the rear.

"I'm...I'm so sorry." Lauren stammered.

"What are you sorry about? You didn't scream, you didn't let go. You did good."

J.P. reassured her. "Spot was trying to keep up with the other horses. I guess Butcher forgot he had a new rider. Alice will give him an ear full when we get back to the stables."

Lauren wiped the tears from her cheeks with the back of her gloved hand.

The rest of the ride was without any incidents. And J.P was correct because Butcher came and apologized to both Lauren and J.P.

On their way back to the city, Lauren said that she wasn't hungry. She just wanted to go home and go to bed.

Under normal circumstances J.P. would have persuaded his date to come to his place. But not with Lauren. He needed time to sort out his tactics. He wanted to- no, needed to- put Lauren in the same category of his past female companions. He had to get control of this aspect of his life. Afterall, he had more important issues than to be tied up with a law student.

"Hey, Lauren, you're home." J.P. said as he gently touched her shoulder.

Slowly, Lauren stretched and yawned before opening her eyes. She turned her head and looked in his direction. An easy smile formed as she looked into his eyes.

"Guess I was tired." she said softly.

"It's okay. You had a rough day."

"I did but it was fun."

"I'm happy to know that. But I need to tell you something. This is going to be a busy week. Landau is having some issues with one of its foreign suppliers. We are in negotiations but I may not be seeing you in the mornings. However, would you be available next Saturday?"

"Yes, I think so." Lauren said now that she was fully awake.

"Great! I'll call you to give you the correct time I'll pick you up."

"Thanks for a fun day. I don't know if I'll be able to survive riding the elevator alone in the mornings." She said with a smile.

J.P. hesitated about getting out of the car to walk Lauren to her door. He feared that his emotions would take control again. He didn't want that!

Lauren eased from the vehicle, gathered her things and walked slowly to her door. She knew he was watching her. She also instinctively knew that he was fighting, having deep feelings for her. But she was willing to be patient. Upon reaching her door, she waved without turning to look back at him.

The following Saturday they were again enjoying the waters of the lake. After swimming for a long while, J P. noticed that clouds were moving in. He told Lauren that they'd better get back on board and head for home. This time as he helped her up onto the deck, she moved in close and kissed him gently. He was surprised, "Are you sure?" he asked.

"Yes." she said before wrapping her arms around his neck.

Their kiss was deep and their hug was tight. Suddenly, a strong wind gust rocked the boat causing them to almost lose their footing.

J.P. looked up, a storm was approaching quickly.

"We'd better get going." he said, releasing his hold on her reluctantly.

"Yes," Lauren was breathless. "I'll go below, get some dry clothes on."

J.P. grabbed his anorak putting it on quickly. The rain was light but he knew it wouldn't be long before it would be dangerous.

Finally, he glided the boat into the slip. Both he and Lauren moved quickly, tying up the boat. Once the boat was secured, he took her hand as they ran to his car. Once in the car, they laughed as they wiped the rain water from their faces.

J.P., finally stopped laughing and asked Lauren if she wanted to eat. She nodded yes. So J.P. got his cell phone and called a seafood restaurant. He ordered 2 trout dinners to be delivered to his place in an hour.

When they arrived at his condo, Lauren was in awe. It was a 2 story condo with the kitchen, living/dining area with a bathroom and small guest room.

Upstairs there was a master bedroom and bath. And two additional bedrooms with a shared bath. He showed her to one of the upstairs bedrooms.

"You can use this room. There are towels and other things you may need."

A half an hour later J.P. was back downstairs, sipping a brandy as he stared out his floor to ceiling living room windows. He was relishing the kiss. He realized that his heart was involved. This wasn't supposed to be and yet he was at the point where he didn't care. All his life he'd kept a schedule and all his success depended on keeping a tight efficient schedule. But now, he didn't care.

"Is the food here yet?" Lauren asked.

J.P. turned around to see a vision of beauty.

Lauren was dressed in a yellow romper and wedge sandals. Her curls were pulled up into high ponytail, large hooped earrings.

J.P. almost dropped his glass as he watched her descend the stairs and approach him. Putting his glass down he walked to her, wrapping his arms around her. He began kissing her forehead, her cheeks then finally her mouth.

The doorbell rang, several times before either of them became aware of the sound. Reluctantly, they separated. J.P. went to the door and intercom while Lauren headed for the kitchen to locate the plates, utensils and glassware.

After their meal, they sat together on the sofa looking out the windows. Lauren's head rested on J.P.'s shoulder with his arm wrapped around hers.

"What kind of music do you like?" J.P. asked.

"I like almost all genres of music. I can find a few tunes that I enjoy listening to. But now with you, sitting here there's one tune that touches my heart."

"Really? What's the name?"

Lauren smiled. "It's called Love's Silhouette by Pieces of a Dream."

J.P. stood up, spoke to the virtual assistant, "Love's Silhouette by Pieces of a Dream." Then he extended his hand to Lauren, "Dance with me."

As the music began, J.P. pulled Lauren close. Gently touching her face with his fingertips he smiled. As they began to dance he whispered into her ear, "You are so lovely."

Lauren's throat tightened as she held back tears. No man had ever said those words to her. She rested her head on his shoulder. Lauren's joy at this moment was indescribable.

The rain had stopped and the sun's rays could be seen as the clouds began to break up. This quiet special moment came to a halt when J.P.'s cell phone vibrated.

"I need to get this." J.P. said after glancing at his phone which was resting on the coffee table. He grabbed the phone as he walked away.

Lauren couldn't understand the conversation but his tone wasn't happy. He seemed irritated with what he was being told.

Fifteen minutes later he completed the call.

"Lauren, I'm sorry but there's a situation with work. I need to go out of town. Would you mind if I take you home now?"

"If it's important, I'll just get home on my own. Public transportation is my friend." she said with a smile. The special mood had been broken.

"Not the way you look today. I don't want some guy flirting with you. I'm paying for a taxi to get you home." J.P. said before pulling her close for another kiss.

Lauren received a text from J.P. on Sunday advising her that he and others were flying to France. And that he would contact her as soon as possible.

By Wednesday she hadn't heard anything. The office gossip was that if the negotiations were successful then Landau would be in the top 100 corporations in the United States. And only the second minority owned company.

Lauren hadn't heard anything. So she decided to go to J.P. place to collect the clothes she'd left there on Saturday. He had been in such a mental state that they both forgot her things from the boat.

Entering the lobby, she approached a gentleman sitting at a raised desk.

"Hi, I need to speak to the housekeeper for 2001. Her name is Petra and she cleans Mr. Paul's place." Lauren said. J.P. had told her on one of their Wednesday lunches that his place gets cleaned by a nice woman named Petra.

The man at the desk looked at her with a puzzled expression. "We don't have a Mr. Paul living in this building. Are you sure you're in the right place?"

"Yes and his housekeeper is named Petra, like I just said."

"Well, yes I know Petra but she cleans for Mr. Landau."

"No, there's some mistake!" Lauren replied.

"No mistake. Tall, good-looking man with a friendly smile."

Lauren stood still as the shock of the reality of her situation hit hard. He'd lied to her. He'd been leading on. She had assumed that his last name was Paul. And that he went by his initials. She'd fallen in love with a liar.

With a quick nod, Lauren turned and left. Anger, hate and pain were the emotions hitting her all at once. "I'll never speak to him again. How can I trust a man who hides his identity?" she said to herself.

On the plane flying back from France J.P. and Allan Hess sat side by side. "This was tough." J.P. said to Allan.

"Yes, but very successful. You're a good negotiator J.P." Allan replied.

"We all did well. And you, with your knowledge of international law, really helped."

"Ever since we've been working on this, I began brushing up."

"It really showed. Everyone on the team did an excellent job." J.P. said as he glanced around the plane at the men and women who'd assisted.

"J.P., I've noticed something different about you over the past couple of months." Allan said.

"Oh, really? What?"

"I can't quite put my finger on it but you don't seem so serious. You've been, I don't know, smiling more."

"I don't think so. It's just that I'm getting out more. Not working like I've done in the past." J.P. said. He was surprised that anyone noticed. He had to admit that since he'd been seeing Lauren, he was happy.

"Well, I'm thinking you've finally met someone." Allan said.

"Maybe, but I'm going to get some shut eye." J.P. said before closing his eyes.

But he couldn't stop his smile.

THIS CAN'T BE!

*L*eaving J.P.'s residence, Lauren immediately phoned Ella advising her that she had an emergency and would not be able to continue her intern-ship. Next she phoned her mother's dearest friend.

Shanell had been Monica's confidant for as long as Lauren could remember. All during Monica's fight with cancer Shanell was a constant presence. She was a second mother. And after Monica's death, she helped Michael with parenting duties. Lauren spent many days talking and sharing things she couldn't talk to her father about.

"Hello Lauren. What's the matter?" Shanell's soft southern voice asked.

"Why does something have to be wrong?" Lauren said before she began crying.

"Lauren, where are you?"

"I'm sitting on a bench near Navy Pier. And I can't seem to stop crying." Lauren sobbed as she spoke.

"Is it a man?"

"Yes, how did you know?"

"Cause it usually is, babe."

"I need to come and stay with you for a while. Would that be possible?"

"Of course."

Lauren hurried home to begin packing. She contacted 2 BFit to ask for a leave of absence. She asked Chris to get in touch with one of the other instructors to cover her classes. Next she called her cell phone provider to have her phone number changed.

Shanell arrived in a timely manner to pick Lauren up. They loaded two large suitcases, one smaller one and a backpack into the truck of the car. After they were on the road, Shanell didn't ask any questions, she waited for Lauren to speak.

"Shanell, can we stop to get something to eat?"

"I've got some gumbo at my house. We'll eat and talk then. Why don't you just close your eyes and rest." Shanell suggested.

Lauren nodded as she stifled a yawn. Closing her eyes Lauren dozed off.

A couple of days later, Lauren's depression had lessened but her disappointment was still crushing. She couldn't understand how she didn't see the signs. She knew that the CEO of Landau and Associates had the same initials. Lauren was determined to purge herself of all feelings for J.P.

For now, Lauren needed to get a job so she was searching on her computer. But her heart wasn't in the job search. So she decided to rent a car and go to visit her grandparents.

As soon as Lauren left for her visit, Shanell made a phone call.

"I just wanted you to know that she's gone to visit her grandparents."

"How long will she be gone?"

"About 4 days. And this is August." Shanell said.

"Do you think she knows?"

"I doubt it. But this is what Monica wanted. And we both promised her when in the month of her death and Lauren's 25th year we'd tell her everything." Shanell said.

Her voice was emotional as she choked back the lump in her throat.

"It will be alright. I'll bring the envelope tomorrow morning. I just hope she won't hate me."

"She loved you once. That seed of love is just buried but when she learns the truth, I think she'll be happy." Shanell said.

They spoke for a few more minutes before disconnecting. Shanell sighed as she walked into her kitchen. She wanted a glass of wine. Thinking about Monica, her dearest friend and of the daughter of a love affair. Yes, Lauren would know everything.

August was difficult for Lauren because it was the month that her mother died. While visiting her grandparents, they reminisce about Monica. Her grandmother recalled the first time they saw Monica at the adoption agency. "It was love at first sight."

Then her grandfather Eddie smiled and nodded in agreement. It was the same story Lauren had heard from her mother. She was found abandoned at a police station. Just a note asking that she be given to a loving family. Being with her grandparents helped Lauren put aside the pain she'd been dealing with. Only at night, just before falling to sleep he'd come to mind. She knew that J.P.'s smile, voice and that wink would always stay with her.

After 4 days Lauren arrived back at Shanell's. She felt somewhat better and was ready to prepare for the bar examination. She knew that she would have to contact the university and Mr. Hess.

When she walked into the house, Shanell called out to her asking to join her in the kitchen. Lauren complied, after putting her luggage in the bedroom.

"Hi, did you enjoy having your house back to yourself?" Lauren teased.

"I missed you. But I have something that I need to give you. I'm going to give you this envelope and I want you to wait before opening it. I'm going to leave you alone while you read the information inside.

I'm also leaving you my car keys just in case you follow the instructions immediately." Then Shanell handed her the white envelope, then with a smile she turned and walked out of the house.

Lauren, bewildered by Shanell's words, slowly opened the sealed envelope. Lauren sat rereading the letter and the attached instructions. *Is this real?* Lauren closed her eyes to think. Her mother's insurance had paid for her funeral and another policy had been divided between herself, her siblings and their father. So where was this coming from?

"My dearest daughter," the letter began.

I had wanted to tell you the truth for so long but always found an excuse not to explain. I then decided to wait until you were 21. Now, however, because of my illness I will not see your twenty-first birthday. I must explain everything. I can only ask that you forgive me and try to understand.

No one is perfect, especially me. But I love you more than any parent should love a child because you were conceived in love.

Michael Boyd is not your birth father. We'd separated because of his drinking and verbal abuse. I had gone to work for a prestigious law firm to support myself and your siblings. I enjoyed the work and your brother and sister were old enough for me to work outside the home. One of the junior partners and I didn't care about each other at first but over time his feelings toward me changed. I tried to maintain a professional attitude but I fell in love with him. Not only was he intelligent, but he was kind and gentle. The complete opposite of Michael.

Unfortunately, I felt obligated to mend my marriage. I had two children to consider. I had married young thinking that I was mature. And Michael and I did love each in a wild youthful kind of love. My parents opposed our relationship but being headstrong Michael and I eloped. And of course in hindsight my parents were right.

The last night with my lover, you were conceived. When I discovered I was pregnant I had returned to Michael. I thought I'd pass you off as Michael's but when you were born, there was nothing of Michael in you. Since I was adopted and didn't know my ancestry, I'd hoped Michael would accept you. He didn't. I explained to him and he became sullen and then angry. I feared that he would revert back to the abuse that had been our former life. Instead, he blamed himself and agreed to raise you as his.

The enclosed photos are of your real father. He loves you very much and he was even present at your birth. Michael happened to be out of town. Your father set up a trust for you.

Enclosed is a key to a bank deposit box. Shanell promised to help you and you can go to the bank where you will glean additional information.'

Lauren was stunned to say the least. The pictures showed her with her mother and a man who looked very familiar. So grabbing Shanell's car keys she headed for the bank. After showing her identification at the bank, Lauren sat in a small room with the deposit box on the wooden table in front of her.

Slowly, she lifted the lid of the box. Inside were photographs of her mother smiling with another man. As she began to look through the pictures Lauren saw herself as an infant and as a toddler. The man was familiar. In the picture where the three of them were together, the man holding her as a toddler in his arms, it was Allan Hess!

Closing her eyes Lauren searched her memory. Those pictures helped to bring to the surface feelings she must have buried. There was also another white envelope with more information. Monica explained that Allan moved away because he couldn't stand being a part-time parent. He continued to send money because Michael couldn't maintain regular employment. 'All your teddy bears, new clothes were from your Dad. Allan loves you and for the first 8 years of your life you called him Uncle Al. When he moved away you would ask about him. You cried when I explained that he'd moved away. You two had such a bond. As a mother, I could see that Michael didn't treat you as kindly as he did your brother and sister. So I worked extra hard to give you more love.'

Now so much made sense. The way Michael made her feel inadequate especially after Monica's death. The additional information explained her silver bear necklace with its inscription. And at the very bottom of the box was a card that read, "To our daughter, from Daddy."

And taped to the card was a small gold ring. Lauren put the ring on her small finger. She recalled that Allan wore a ring on the small finger of his left hand. Gathering all the pictures and letters she carefully placed everything into a large cloth bag the bank had provided. She had a lot to think about and she wanted to contact her Dad.

J.P. LANDAU

*A*ll J.P. could think about was Lauren. The trip overseas had been exhausting but it had been a success. How he would be successful explaining his deception to Lauren?

Growing up in a middle class working family, J.P. had always wanted to be rich. In his teen years he maintained a 4.0 grade point average. While in college he carried a double major of business management and computer science. It was in his senior year that he met Glen.

It was in the beginning of that year, they were taking 3 classes together. Glen, very cordial, asked if they could study together. He was struggling with one of financial classes. Studying together, they discovered that they both enjoyed biking.

It was during spring break that Glen invited J.P to meet his family. Glen was the youngest of 4. His parents were wealthy and both were active in real estate and the stock market. J.P. having come from modest means was overwhelmed by the opulence the Glen took for granted.

Glen's family lived in one of the northern suburbs of Chicago with their lakefront property. While out riding bikes J.P. couldn't stop speaking of the beauty of the house and the surrounding property.

"Yeh, it's okay but I just want a little bit of a simpler life. My older brother is just like my dad. Greed is their life blood. My other brother is into conservation. So the conversation when we're together can get pretty heated." Glen said. He and J.P. were taking a break from the ride.

"What about you and your sister?" J.P. asked.

"Cheryl is a research doctor and she loves it. As for me, I want to own a couple of franchises, get married and have a family."

"Not me, I want to be like your Dad and brother," J.P. exclaimed.

"I thought so. That's one reason I invited you here. I've told my folks a little of your aspirations. And well, they want to talk to you."

"Really! Why would they want to help me?" J.P. asked.

"They have a philanthropic attitude. They help many minority organizations anonymously. They both want to hear about your plans, you know, your dreams to acquire wealth,"

Now here he was in his early 30's and worth more than he'd ever dreamed. But he wasn't as happy as he thought. He wanted to share his life with someone he loved. Now that love had come unexpectedly. He realized that he wanted what Glen had. A family of his own and maybe even children. But most of all he wanted Lauren.

When he returned to the United States his first call was to her. But he couldn't connect. He phoned Allan Hess' secretary where he found out that she'd quit. Then he phoned 2BFit, and spoke with Chris who told him that she'd disappeared. That Jeanette didn't even know where she was.

"Can you give me Jeanette's number?" J.P. asked, his tone angry.

"Hey now J.P. it's not Jeanette's fault that Lauren has disappeared. What did you do?" Chris said,

Realizing how he was sounding, J.P. apologized. "It's just that I need to explain things to her. I messed up."

"Ok but know that Jeanette is having a hard time with this also. I do know that she's spoken to Lauren once but that's all." Then Chris gave J.P. the number. With words of gratitude and apologizing again J.P. terminated their conversation.

"Hello, Jeanette, it's J.P. Do you have time to talk?"

"I guess. I just got this text from Chris letting me know you'd be calling. I'm angry with you because you've broken my best friend's heart. Did you know she cried almost throughout our entire conversation?" Jeanette's anger was palpable.

"You're right and I'm so very sorry. I need to talk to her."

"Well, you can't. She changed her number and I don't have it. She used a burner phone when she called."

"Will you be speaking with her again?" J.P. asked hopefully.

"Yes, she'll probably call me again. But why should I help you?" Jeanette asked, her tone cool.

"Because I realized that I love her. I want to make amends. Make things right. So please, when you talk with her again tell,…no ask her to give me a chance. I'll explain everything to her." Silence.

"Jeanette are you there?" J.P. asked.

"Yes, I'm just wondering how sincere you are?"

"Believe me, I've never in my life been more sincere." J.P. said.

"Okay, you sound sincere. When I hear from her, I'll tell her what you said. But I still don't trust you. I've got to go now." Then the phone went dead.

J.P sighed as he looked at the now silent cell phone. Jeanette was his only possible link to Lauren. He could only hope.

As the days passed, riding the elevator alone now was difficult. He would recall their brief morning conversations and their parting words, "Make your day great." And how she'd bring one of her homemade muffins or a chocolate chip cookie. But what stood out in his memory were their lunches. The laughter, her smile with that small gap in her top teeth. He loved that about her. And even though they'd only kissed a few times, those kisses were burned in his mind and heart. He needed more.

ALLAN HESS

I t had been 3 days since he'd taken the envelope to Shanell. And yet he hadn't heard anything from Lauren. Did she hate him that much? When he contacted Shanell all she said was to be patient. He'd been patient for almost 20 years. He wanted to get to know his daughter not just from photographs, or as her college instructor. All he had had was 8 years of personal time with Lauren and Monica.

After Lauren had turned 8 years old, he was concerned. Michael had been an over the road truck driver. That allowed him, Monica and Lauren to spend many days together. However, Michael was tired of driving claiming that he was missing being home with his family. Allan suspected that Michael knew more than he was saying.

One day at Lincoln Park Zoo, Monica told him that Michael had given his two week notice.

"He's going to become a diesel mechanic." she'd said. "He'll be home every evening and weekend."

All Allan could do was hug Monica. But he knew that he'd have to make a decision.

He'd been offered a partnership with a law firm in Springfield. He had been procrastinating on making a decision. Now even though it would break his heart he knew that he'd have to leave.

That was the past. Mistakes, bad decisions had been made. If he had to do it over again, he would somehow take his daughter. But the saying that "children need their mother". Is that true? Allan wondered if he would have been a good single father. Just then his phone beeped. It was a number he didn't recognize. Could it be Lauren?

"Hello," Allan said.

"It's Lauren. We need to talk." her voice soft hesitating between each word.

"Yes, yes we do. When can we get together?"

"Lincoln Park Zoo by the bears." Lauren said.

"Of course! What day and time?" Allan said, trying not to sound too eager.

"Saturday morning at 11:00. And can I call you Allan?"

"Yes, that would be fine."

"Good, I'll see you then." The phone went dead before Allan could say anything else.

But she had called. He smiled as he poured himself a brandy. Sitting in his easy chair he felt overjoyed with the possibility of finally having his daughter.

ALLAN AND LAUREN

It was very humid Saturday but the zoo was busy. Allan stood by the brown bear enclosure. He didn't want to be late. This was too important. Dressed in taupe linen slacks, off-white cotton shirt and light blue cap he began to pace. He glanced at his watch then checked the time on his cell phone. It was 10:55.

Lauren watch Allan from a distance. She'd arrived 30 minutes early. She wanted to see him not as her university instructor or her boss at the law firm. Lauren truly wanted to see the man whom her mother had loved.

Calling out Lauren approached him. When they got close they stared at each other. Then Lauren made the first move, she just hugged him. They both cried.

Allan, after all these years finally was holding his daughter again.

For Lauren, holding on to her real father made her feel joy. At this moment she remembered his fragrance. This triggered a long lost memory. It was Uncle Al's scent.

A clean, cool fragrance.

"I remember!" Lauren exclaimed as she released her hug.

"Remember what?" Allan said as he took a step back.

"All the photos that mom left of us caused me to recall part of my past. But hugging you now, awakened in me a feeling of security. As a kid you'd hold me and say lovely words or sing to me. Your fragrance. It's what I've missed."

"I've worn this same fragrance for years and you remember." Allan said in disbelief.

Lauren just nodded. She couldn't speak. All the years of feeling unloved after the death of her mother. Trying so hard to please the man she thought was her father. Now she knew with certainty, Michael never loved her. He couldn't because she was a constant reminder of a dark period of his marriage to Monica, the woman he loved.

"Let's walk and talk a little." Allan suggested.

Lauren nodded again and they began walking side by side. After a few minutes, Lauren slipped her hand into his. Allan's heart swelled with joy as he gently squeezed his daughter's hand just as he used to do when she was a child.

Allan shared some of his memories of their times together. Not only going to the zoo but window shopping, and amusement parks. But their picnics were for him the best times.

"But how did we get together without my brother and sister?" Lauren asked.

"Before you began school, it was easy. Your siblings would be in school, Michael was on the road so we could be together. When you started school, we basically had the weekends and sometimes your brother and sister would be with us. Especially if we went to the movies."

"But didn't Tamara or Tony wonder who you were?" Lauren asked.

"Remember your siblings are a lot older than you. And Shanell helped. Somehow we were able to see each other. However, when Michael decided to quit driving over the road that's when I left."

"Yes, I recall missing you so much. And I got mad because I thought I'd done something to make you stop coming over." Lauren said.

"I'm sorry. sweetheart but I couldn't deal with the idea of living in the same city and not seeing you." Allan admitted.

Their conversation continued over lunch at a nearby restaurant. By 3:00 they decided to part with plans to see each other the next day.

"Allan, you're my father but the word father seems too formal to me. I'd like to call you dad but since I call Michael dad I don't want to use that for you. Could I call you Pops?" Lauren said.

Allan didn't answer immediately. He thought about it.

"Pops it is. Yes, I like it! Oh, one more thing. You are named after my mother. Your full name is Lauren Alexis Hess."

"Yes and this week I'll be getting my last name changed to Hess." Lauren beamed.

With a final hug they parted knowing that their future would be wonderful.

J.P. no longer got to work early. Riding the elevator alone in the mornings brought back too many memories. "It's strange," he thought one evening as he sat looking out of the windows of his living room, "three mornings a week for about 2 months, lunches, bike rides, a horseback ride and a few kisses. And I can't get her out of my mind, or my heart." Standing up abruptly, he made up his mind to hire a private detective. He needed to find Lauren no matter the cost.

The days and weeks passed and although Lauren was enjoying her new job and preparing for the bar exam, J.P. was still part of her. No matter how hard she tried, she missed him. But now she was also fearful that his feelings for her had faded. Afterall, she thought it was the middle of September and he probably was dating someone new.

Allan's parental love for Lauren was over the moon. He couldn't do enough for her. It was as if he was making up for the years he wasn't with her.

"Pops, I really don't need anything." Laureen said in a sincere yet serious tone. "I'm still staying with Shanell without paying rent.

You helped me get a position with a good law firm. I just enjoy being with you, getting better acquainted with a parent who has loved me without me knowing it. So really, I'm good."

"I just enjoy making you smile but okay. But I want to give you one more thing. You need a car." Allan said.

"Pops, I live in the city. Public transportation and my bicycle suit me just fine."

"But what about the times you go visit your grandparents or come to my place. Or don't you ever just want to go for a drive?"

"Well, yes at times but I usually rent a car." Lauren said. Although she'd been thinking of getting a car. It was tiring waiting for the bus. "Okay, Pops to be honest I would like a car. I do like the Mini Coopers."

"Great, great! We can go this weekend." Allan beamed as he rubbed the palms of his hands together.

That weekend Lauren became the proud owner of a blue Mini.

Getting to know her father filled the void Lauren had missed. Now her life was so much better. The pains of feeling unloved by a man who's supposed to love you unconditionally but instead had ignored her. And more so after the death of her mother.

How many times through her teen years did she cry tears of loneliness and anger.

Michael would just glare at her whenever she attempted to share any of her academic achievements. His attitude made her feel so inadequate. It was the strength of her mother's love that sustained her. And also a subconscious feeling of joy and love from her distant childhood.

Now being with Allan, her Pops, it was him. It was his joy and loving kindness that she had now rediscovered. And Allan's feelings for her were now coming into her consciousness. As they reminisced their times together during Lauren's early years they would laugh and at times cry. Monica was always a part of their discussions.

Allan was dating a woman named Betty. She was a widow with a grown son. "She's nice," Allan explained to Lauren, "and I want you to get to know her. I've been single for a very long time.

We met at a gala over a year ago. We have many things in common. We both love pickleball, golf and watching the Chicago Bulls. Plus other things."

"Have you told her about me and my mother?" Lauren asked. They were walking in Grant Park. It was a cool September day.

"Yes, and she wants to meet you." Allan seemed to blush slightly.

"Then of course, I'd love to meet her. After all, I must see if she's bonafide." Lauren said with a chuckle.

Allan smiled as he hugged his daughter around her shoulders.

J.P. AND ALLAN

*A*llan was at work looking over some legal papers that he needed to present to J.P. and other executives. He thought he'd never be so happy again in his life. He and Lauren were closer than ever. When she met Betty, Lauren was surprised that Betty was Nigerian.

Lauren even commented that she could pass as their biological daughter. That seemed to break any possible tension. Allan had a meal of roasted chicken, rice, and candied sweet potatoes. Betty brought greens and Lauren made cheesecake. It was for Allan one of many joyful memories he could hold close to his heart.

He had loved Monica with a passion that was beyond words. And he knew that if she were alive, somehow they would have married. But, with Betty his love was mature and fulfilling. They were good together. And with his daughter back in his life things couldn't be better.

"Allan, J.P. is here. He wants to talk to you." Ella said over the intercom.

"Of course." Allan was surprised that J.P. was at his office.

"Hey Allan, I've been wanting to talk to you for sometime. But I've been embarrassed so I have just buried myself in work. Do you have time to talk?" J.P. asked.

"Sure, let's sit over here on the couch." Allan said as he stood and moved from behind his desk.

Allan took a corner of the couch while J.P. sat down on the edge of the cushion on the other end. Allan studied the young executive's face and could see tension. "Was there something wrong with the company?" Allan wondered as he waited for J.P. to speak.

"Allan, earlier this summer you had a young woman working as an intern. Her name was Lauren Boyd." J.P. said as he wrung his hands together.

"Yes, she was an excellent worker."

"I'm trying to find her." J.P.'s voice remorseful.

"Why?" Allan asked. His curiosity peaked.

"I love her. That is, I fell in love with her." J.P. exhaled deeply. It was the first time he'd said those words out loud. "I'm hiring a private detective to hopefully locate her. I was hoping you had some information that might help."

Silence. Allan focused on J.P.'s demeanor before saying anything. Shanell had mentioned some time ago that Lauren was hurting over some man. So this must be the man.

"J.P. over all the years we've known each other you've never been serious about any woman. I remember you saying, what was it? Oh, yes PPF wasn't that your saying?" Allan's tone, cool and calm.

"Yes, and I hate to admit it but yes. I'm all about scheduling and this wasn't in my plans." J.P. stood and began to pace.

As Allan watched J.P. he debated whether to let him hire the detective or let him know where Lauren was. He liked J.P. and he couldn't in good conscience let him suffer any more.

"J.P. sit down please. Before you hire that P.I we need to talk. What I have to tell you will take awhile. Do you have plans for this evening?"

"Well, no not really. I was just going to work late and head home."

"I've got to finish this work. So why don't you come over to my place at about 6:30? I'll order pizza and you bring the beer" Allan said.

"You can't tell me now?" J.P. asked.

"No, so will you come?"

"Yes, what choice do I have?"

Allan stood and walked J.P. to the door. "I'll see you later."

Allan said as he ushered J.P. out of his office. After closing the door Allan slowly shook his head as he returned to his desk. This is going to be an interesting evening, he thought.

After stopping at the liquor store J.P. headed north to the suburb of Evanston. This community was the home of Northwestern University. It was clean and quiet with many of its streets tree lined. J.P thought with the money Allan earned he would live in the city in an exclusive high rise. Afterall, he was a bachelor so why would he prefer a house? J.P. drove his vehicle into the side driveway behind Allan's car.

As soon as J.P. approached the front door, he heard Allan yelling that the door was unlocked and to come in.

"I'm in the kitchen, come on back." Allan's voice sounded cheerful.

"Hey, I made it. I got two different 6 packs of beer. I didn't know which was your favorite." J.P. said as he placed the bottles on the counter top.

"As long as they are in bottles. I hate canned beer. So you did great." Allan said. "Put them in the fridge. The pizza will be here soon. Why don't we open a couple of bottles and we can sit and talk."

The two men sat down at the oval shaped kitchen table. J.P. glanced around the pale gray walled kitchen with white cabinets. He noticed the accent colors were yellow.

"I'm not much on decorating but your kitchen looks nice." J.P. said.

"Thanks but I can't take credit. I had an interior designer do it. He asked me what colors I liked. I told him gray, blue, green and tan. This house had been abandoned and the previous resident hadn't been able to take very good care of it. Anyway it took awhile to gut it. But I like it."

Before J.P. could comment, the doorbell sounded and Allan got up to answer the door.

After placing the large deep dish pizza in the middle of the table, he handed a sanitizing cloth to J.P. to cleanse his hands. Then the bell rang again. This time a lovely mature woman entered the kitchen. Her hair was in a beautiful headwrap, she wore an over-sized white shirt and jeans.

"J.P. I want you to meet Shanell. She's part of Lauren's life that you need to know about." Allan said.

"Ahh, you're the young man my girl is trying so hard to for-get." Shanell said as she extended her hand to J.P.

"Your girl? I don't understand." J.P. stammered.

"Between Shanell and I you'll understand Lauren. So let's get to eating and talking." Allan said as he grabbed a wine glass to give to Shanell.

Once seated Shanell pulled from her tote bag a bottle of wine explaining to J.P. that she liked wine with pizza, not beer.

Between bites of pizza and sips of brew Allan explained how he met Monica. How their friendship grew into love. "I was just a young attorney working for a law firm on the northside of Chicago. One of the secretaries went on maternity leave and Monica came in as a temp." Allan paused for a moment remembering the first time he saw her. "I didn't want to be attracted to her so I was sarcastic and demanding. She didn't seem to get angry. Finally, after about 3 or 4 months we had some work that needed to be completed and ended up working late. After we finished I offered to buy dinner. She seemed to hesitate before accepting."

Shanell picked up the story as Allan ate some food. "Monica shared with me how this young arrogant attorney had been treating her at first. But for some reason, he'd changed. And her feelings had also changed. Their feelings for each other were growing into love. Monica wanted to stay faithful to Michael. However, he was gone for a long time. And when he was home he'd drink in excess." "So they became lovers?" J.P. said.

"In a word, yes. But not the jumping in the bed lovers. Monica was cautious.

And I was willing to wait. She was conflicted. She was married and had two children. Then Michael quit the over the road job. He began working for a local trucking company."

"But why did she stay married to Michael?" J.P. asked

"I think she felt a sense of duty or obligation. Michael was her first love. For many women, the first man they are intimate with, the woman feels a special bond. And for Monica, because of the children she had to make the marriage work," Shanell said. She continued, "We had long talks about her and Allan. And then her and Michael. Allan was everything she'd wanted Michael to be. Monica's emotions were on a roller coaster ride."

Allan looked surprised when he heard that.

"We'd steal time during the weekdays with Michael being on the road so we could be together some evenings. Shanell would babysit her children. It was hard on both of us. So I made the decision to leave the law firm and go elsewhere. That was the day Lauren was conceived. A couple of months later Monica told me she was pregnant.

I had to stay close. For the eight years after Lauren's birth I was available as much as possible. It's crazy, I know. But Monica didn't want Tony and his sister to be traumatized by divorce of their parents."

"Yes, she was conflicted." Shanell chimed in, "We had long conversations. But I also think she liked the thrill of having a secret love. Anyway, by the time Lauren was eight, Allan knew he couldn't wait any longer."

"Eight years!" J.P. gasped.

Allan nodded. "Yes, but I was with my child whom I loved more than anything. Then Michael decided to work where he'd be home more. That was a wake-up call for me. I took an offer in Springfield."

"Was Monica that beautiful? I mean 8 years is an awful long time." J.P. said.

"For me she was intoxicating." Allan admitted.

"Monica wasn't a flirt but when she was any place men couldn't help themselves. But there was a sweetness about her so other women couldn't hate her. Lauren has some of that." Shanell said.

"Yes she does." Allan agreed.

The conversation continued as the pizza and liquor were consumed.

"I understand more about Lauren. So how do I get her back? How can I have her trust me again?" J.P. asked.

"We have a plan."

THE PLAN

Two days later J.P. was still working on how this plan would work. He usually maintained a low profile. J.P. had gotten into the habit of sending one of his top executives to fundraisers or high profile gallery openings. Whenever he received an invitation, he'd have Esther recruit a V.P. from a department to represent Landau & Associates.

He was home, alone as usual listening to jazz music when a song came on that caused him to think of Lauren. The song title, 'You Make Me Smile," touched his heart. He recalled her smile many times throughout each day. He also played Love Silhouette by Pieces of a Dream. That was the last time he'd held her close. Now all he had were those memories and a pink and white bag with Lauren's swimsuit. She never returned to get her items.

It was sometime later that his housekeeper, Petra, asked about the items that had been left in the guest room. Reluctantly, he reached for his phone. He phoned Shanell explaining that Lauren had left her bag.

"I don't know how I can get this back to her." J.P. said.

"Just give it to Allan. He can just tell her that you found it and thought he'd have a better chance of getting it to her."

"Okay, but I'm still not comfortable with this plan. I usually keep a low profile."

Next he phoned Glen to ask for his sister Cheryl's phone number. Glen was curious and was cautious about giving J.P. her number. J.P. explained briefly why he wanted to talk to Cheryl. Glen, after learning of the plan, gave J.P. Cheryl's number with specific orders that Cheryl understood the goal.

Lauren was returning to work after her lunch when she heard someone calling her name. At first she ignored it but after a third shout out which was closer, she turned around.

"Hey, you!"

"Oh my! Marcus!" Lauren exclaimed.

"I thought it was you. I was across the street and well I noticed your hair." he said with a smile.

"Is my hair that weird?"

"No but it's the copper highlights that mix with dark brown and those corkscrew curls. I hoped it was you." Marcus said.

"Well, how are you? Do you work around here?"

"No, but I had some business in the area. And there's this deli that makes the best ham and cheese on rye in the city. So I was on my way there to get lunch. What about you?"

"I work at a small law firm not too far from here. I'm on my way back to the office." Lauren said.

"This may sound crazy but I'd hoped to see you again. Everytime I jog along the drive I notice the bench where we met. But I guess that guy on the bike is someone special. He didn't look too happy that I was speaking with you." Marcus said.

"Oh, yes, well he's just a friend. I think he was just being overly protective." Lauren said although that wasn't exactly the truth.

"I won't keep you but could we exchange contact information? I'd like to call you."

Lauren hesitated for a moment but then agreed. After they exchanged information, Lauren rushed to work. As she headed for her office she thought J.P. is out of my life. *I need to move on. Marcus seems nice.* Yet she felt guilty as if she were betraying her heart.

A couple of days later, Marcus called and they made plans for lunch that coming Saturday.

"Shanell, I'm leaving now."

"Okay, is this with this Marcus guy?"

"Yes. Do you need anything while I'm out?" Lauren asked.

"No but before you go look at this. There was a big event at one of the hotels. And isn't this the guy Allan works for?" Shanell held up her cell phone Lauren could see the picture of J.P. with a lovely brunette.

Lauren felt a restriction near her heart. J.P. looked as handsome as ever. He was smiling but it wasn't the smile she saw when they were together.

"And look, here's your father with Betty. Don't they look good together?"

"Yes." Lauren said as she turned and with a quick wave left the house.

"She still has feelings for him." Shanell said quietly.

MARCUS AND LAUREN

Lunch was at a 50's style diner located south of downtown. The place was very busy but they got a booth in the back. Water and menus were placed on the table as soon as they got seated. Then the waitress said she would be back.

"This is an interesting place." Lauren said as she looked around. Red. black and white with chrome was the decor. The level of noise and conversation was good. And from what Lauren saw, the food portions were generous.

"Have you eaten here before?" Lauren asked.

"Yes, this is one of my favorite places. The prices aren't bad and the food is great." Marcus said with a smile.

"Is there anything special you'd recommend?"

"I'm a breakfast eater. So I usually get something from that menu. But please get anything you want,"

As Lauren studied the menu her mind wandered back to her first date with J.P.

She'd paid for the meal, and how easy it was to talk to him.

"So have you decided?" Marcus asked bringing Lauren back to the present.

"Oh, yes. I'll go with a hamburger and fries."

The waitress returned and Marcus placed both orders.

"So are you a law clerk?" Marcus asked as he leaned back onto the red cushions.

"In a way, but I will graduate soon. Then I'll be an attorney if I pass the bar exam."

"Nice." Marcus nodded.

"And what about you? Did you mention that you work from home."

Marcus began explaining the nuances of his job. He works for a California based company. He explained that he primarily handled payroll, pay raises and insurance benefits for all the employees. It was fairly easy but any new business that the salespeople signed up it was his job to enter that new employee or client's information into the computer system.

"Is it a growing business?" Lauren asked.

"Yes and since it's in California there are many environmental concerns that need to be met."

Soon the waitress brought their food. As they ate they learned a little more about each other. Marcus was from Chicago and had attended school on the westside. After high school he'd gone to a community college for a couple of years. While attending college he became involved with some students who were extremely prejudiced.

"I was part of some demonstrations. There's so much bias in this country." He said with an angry tone.

"Do you still have those feelings?" Lauren asked.

"Not like I did. But I do have strong negative feelings when I see a black man with a white or Hispanic woman. I think they are betraying our race."

"Marcus, look at me. I'm a blend. My father is white and as for my mother she didn't know her ancestry. So why are you with me?" Lauren's tone was intense.

"I don't want to make you angry. You can't help who your parents are. But you can decide who you want to be with." Marcus said firmly.

Lauren looked at him with concern. She'd never known anyone who was truly prejudiced. Her mother and grandparents had always told her that there was good and bad in all races. Look at each individual, find the positive or good in each.

Now she was looking at Marcus and what good did she see? Was this an aspect of his personality that she would feel comfortable with? Lauren felt a little uneasy but she did not want to be too judgemental.

As they ate, Lauren changed the subject asking him about his jogging.

"It's going great! I have a buddy who goes running with me 3 to 4 mornings a week. I still want to do a half marathon." Marcus beamed. "And what about you? Are you still riding your bike?"

"Yes, I've been increasing my distances gradually. But I don't go over by the lake very much. I moved a few weeks ago. However, there's a nice park close by and the street traffic isn't too dangerous if I get up early enough." Lauren said before taking a bite into her food.

Their conversation stayed on neutral subjects. Lauren had to ruminate on Marcus' attitude regarding race. She had never understood how someone could hate another because of the outward appearance of that person. She recalled her mother saying

"…that's not part of my DNA."

After their meal, Marcus drove her home which was now located on the south shore area of Chicago. At one time this area had been the home of affluent doctors but it was now a quiet middle class residential area. This was the area that Lauren had called home growing up. Her former home wasn't very far from where she now resided.

"Thanks," Lauren said after Marcus stopped the car in front of Shanell's house. "It was nice."

"I hope I didn't put you off with what I said about interracial dating." Marcus said.

"Well, to be honest I was surprised. I mean sometimes you find yourself attracted to someone who comes from a different culture. Think about this. How about if you were attracted to a woman who was East Indian. Her skin tone could be dark brown but she isn't African-American."

Marcus didn't respond immediately. He seemed surprised.

"I haven't considered that," he said.

Lauren began to exit the 2-door compact. "Well, it's food for thought."

"Lauren, could we go out again? Maybe a movie?"

"Give me a call. I like movies." She said before closing the car door.

As Lauren walked toward the house she was listening to hear the car drive away, but it didn't. That is, not until she'd entered the dwelling. After closing the door she leaned her back against it. She thought about Marcus and the fact he was only the second man she had ever dated. Yet, J.P. was the only man she desired to be with.

Shaking her head as if she could remove J.P from her mind she walked into the living room to find her dad, Betty and Shanell. They were playing cards while music was in the background.

"How was your date?" Allan asked.

"How did you know I was on a date?" Lauren asked.

Allan with a smile tilted his head toward Shanell. Lauren turned her attention toward Shanell who just shrugged her shoulders.

Sighing Lauren just said it was interesting. And after giving her father a peck on his cheek she excused herself and went to her room. She wanted to think about Marcus. He seemed nice but her gut was telling her that something wasn't quite right. *Am I comparing him to J.P.?* Lauren wondered. She decided that she needed to talk to Jeanette. It had been awhile and she missed their daily visits.

"Hello, Jeanette. How are you doing?" Lauren said after Jeanette's greeting.

"Lauren! It's about time you called. I've been worried about you. Do you have a permanent cell number now?" Jeanette asked.

"Yes, and this number is it. I've just been so busy and I have so much to tell you. When can we get together?"

"Well, Chris and I have plans for early tomorrow morning. So I should be home anytime after 2."

"You aren't an early morning person. What caused the change?"

"Well it's kind of your fault." Jeanette said with a smile.

"My fault! What do you mean?"

"You remember the first time Chris met J.P. and they went to that upscale bike shop?"

"Yes, I remember that." Lauren said softly.

"So Chris has been on a tear to get a really nice bike. He couldn't afford one that was super expensive but he wanted a good bike. Long story short J.P. has hired Chris to work at Landau. Then he gave him a bonus with the stipulation that Chris will work for him for at least 2 years." Jeanette explained.

"But Chris doesn't graduate until the end of this year."

"Right, but now J.P., Chris, and a guy named Glen have been riding together. Part of me thinks J.P. really wants to help Chris and yet, I think J.P. hopes he can find you through Chris." Jeanette said.

After a few moments of silence Lauren asked if J.P. really wanted to find her.

"So you've seen J.P.?" Lauren asked.

"Yes. And he's not as happy as he was when he was with you."

"But you saw us together once."

"Yeah, I know. But the way he looked at you. I could just see he was enamored with you."

"I really need to talk with you face to face. So tomorrow I'll come over to your place." Lauren said.

After speaking with Jeanette, Lauren sitting cross leg on her bed meditated on her feelings regarding J.P. He hadn't really lied about his identity, it was more of a deception.

But why had he done that? There must have been a reason, but what?

Then Lauren began doing a mental review of her life. Her mother didn't tell her who her real father was. That was deception. Michael had always treated her as an unwanted stepchild only pretending to care. Again deception! And now J.P., could she trust him? Should she give J.P. a chance to explain? *I'll ask my Pops, he knows J.P.* Lauren thought.

Laurn's phone vibrated, it was Marcus.

"Hey, I didn't want to wait a couple of days. I enjoyed being with you. I was wondering if you had plans for tomorrow?" Marcus asked.

"As a matter of fact I do have plans for tomorrow. I'm visiting my dear friend." Lauren said.

"Well, okay. How about next Friday night?"

"I don't have any plans. Yeah, that would be fine." Lauren said.

"Great, I'll pick you up around 6:30."

Lauren arrived promptly at 2:00 to her former dwellings. She'd found a parking spot just a block away. It had been weeks since she'd seen Jeanette. She still had the keys to gain entrance to the building. But she stood in front of the apartment door and she knocked.

Flinging open the door Jeanette squealed with joy, hugging Lauren tightly.

"Girl, I'm so happy to see you. Come in, come in."

"I've missed you so much." Lauren said as she walked into familiar surroundings.

Everything looked the same with the exception of some colorful pillows. Jeanette had the coffee table set with snacks.

"This looks so nice. I didn't mean for you to go to any trouble." Lauren said.

"No trouble. I wanted to. Now what do you want to drink?"

"Cranberry juice."

The two friends got comfortable on the sofa. It was as if no time had passed.

Lauren began explaining in detail the relationship she was building with her real father.

From her tote bag she showed photos of herself, her mother and Allan, her real father. After Jeanette stopped going "Oh my goodness" and "are you kidding me!" Lauren explained exactly who Shenell was.

"You mean to say Shenell knew everything even about your real father and never said a thing?" Jeanette asked.

"Yes, but she'd never met him that is not until after my mother's death. Mother swore her to secrecy." Lauren sighed before taking a drink of the juice. She felt good telling her best friend everything.

"So Michael wasn't your birth father. But because of his love for your mother and maybe blaming himself he supported you." Jeanette said out loud reviewing Laurens information.

"I guess. I'd have to ask him. But honestly I don't care. He wasn't a loving father. Even with my brother and sister he wasn't very affectionate."

"I thought I had it rough." Jeanette said.

"What do you mean?"

"I've never told you this but I got pregnant while in my teens. The father was a guy from a well to do family. We thought that we loved each other. And I guess we did but we were young. Anyway his family wanted me to get an abortion. I just couldn't do that! My father was very angry with me. Called me all kinds of names while my mother tried protecting me.

One evening my mother had gone to the store. My father was in a foul mood and he came into my room with a belt. He began beating me with that belt!" Jeanette's voice was filled with anger. "I tried to escape but he was fast and full of liquor. I lost my baby, my parents got divorced and my young man, his parents moved out of state. I never heard from him."

"So is that why you said those things about J.P.?" Lauren asked.

There was a pause as Jeanette looked at her friend. "Yes, I guess so." she said. "I'm sorry that I judged him without knowing him. He's really not too bad."

"Are telling me that you've talked to J.P."

"Yes. For that matter I was with him, Chris and Glen. We went biking." Jeanette said.

Lauren was speechless.

"I haven't told you because you were so hurt and angry at first. And I was in agreement with you. Then he got my number from Chris. He called me numerous times. He sounded so sincere. And then you kept getting different phone numbers and we really haven't talked until today." Jeanette explained. "You're right. I'm a mess but he's dating other women. So I guess he's over me." Lauren said with a sad voice.

"I don't think so." Jeanette said.

"Really?"

"I think he is just putting up a front. You know, pretending"

"Well, he can keep pretending. I'm seeing someone now." Lauren said, attempting to sound confident.

"You be careful. I almost lost Chris because of pride. And you set me straight. J.P. is good but he will be better with you in his life."

Lauren looked at her friend and saw that she was serious. Lauren relaxed back onto the sofa. Marcus was nice but there were no sparks. With J.P. she would tingle. His voice, smile, the way he would look into her eyes and whenever he'd touch her ever so slightly her heart would race. But Lauren didn't want to yield to those feelings. The only thing she knew for sure was that Allan Hess was her father and he loved her. That she had the love of grandparents, siblings and friends. And although her mother loved her, there had been deceit.

Lauren wanted more time to sort out her feelings. She'd never been in love. She needed to be sure that her feelings for J.P were true and not just physical.

The apartment doorbell rang and Jeanette jumped to answer it.

"It's Chris." Jeanett announced. "He's been wanting to see you. I told him you were coming over."

"Is it just Chris?" Lauren feared that J.P. may be with him.

"He's alone."

Lauren breathed a sigh of relief although she didn't know why.

When Chris came in he gave Jeanette a sweet kiss and then headed straight for Lauren. Lauren had barely stood when he grabbed her with a bear hug.

"I've missed you so much." he said before putting her down.

"I've missed you too. Jeanette has filled me in on what's been happening with your career." Lauren said as she settled back down on the couch.

Chris sat down next to her while Jeanette sat on his other side. Chris explained how J.P. helped him get the internship. And how Landau and Associates is one of the best companies to work for. He could not stop praising J.P. and the team of people that he worked with.

"So you left 2BFit?" Lauren asked.

"Yes, about 3 weeks ago. Derek wasn't happy but he understood. Or so he said. I think he's still angry with you."

"Yes, I can imagine." Lauren said.

"Are you doing okay? Are you happy?" Chris asked with a sincere voice.

"Yes, I'm fine. Just still sorting some things out."

The three friends talked for hours and ordered pizza delivery. Lauren felt happy being with old friends in familiar surroundings. It was almost ten o'clock when Lauren decided she better leave.

"Wait." Jeanette said. "We've got something to tell you." Lauren looked puzzled at her friends.

"We're getting married!" Chris almost shouted.

"OMG!" Lauren said, "And you're just now telling me!" "But I didn't see an engagement ring." Lauren said.

"I don't want one. I told Chris I just want a white gold band with inlaid pink baguette diamonds."

"That sounds lovely." Lauren said, still stunned by the announcement.

"And of course you are going to be my maid-of- honor, that is if you want to."

"Want to, of course I want to." Lauren said hugging her friend and then hugging Chris.

Lauren didn't leave until after midnight. Jeanette tried to get her to stay over but Lauren opted to go. Jeanette made her promise to call when she was safely home.

Driving home the traffic was light. Lauren's thoughts drifted to her conversation with her friends. It would seem that J.P. wasn't deceitful, just cautious. But Lauren didn't want to be wrong. She wanted to stay angry with him. Her life was filled with people not being honest. Why couldn't she have had a normal family? Why couldn't her real father be married to her mother? Why did she have to be an illegitimate child? Why didn't her mother or Michael tell her the truth?

As she parked in front of Shanell's house tears were running down her cheeks. Wiping the tears away with her hands, she killed the engine and got out of her car. The house was almost completely dark except for the hall light. Shanell is probably awake, Lauren thought as she quietly entered the home.

"Is that you, Lauren?" Shanell called from her room.

"Yes, and I'm sorry to be so late,"

"You're a grown woman with your own life. But next time, call me."

"I will." Lauren smiled as she made her way to her room. She felt a headache coming on. And she just wanted to sleep.

J.P. LANDAU

All I want is to be rich, J.P. wrote in his journal at 13 years old. J.P. shut his eyes reminiscing over his teen years. He had studied hard to maintain a high grade point average. His family had moved from England to Chicago before he was ten years old. His father worked as a welder until he got injured. By then J.P. was in his teens. And he began working at a retail store in the shipping department. With his father's injury J.P. wanted to help with the household expenses. Although his mother worked in the public library and a waitress a couple evening a weeks, money was tight.

His younger sisters Donell and Sonja did their part by caring for their father, cooking many of the meals and cleaning the house. During the school year J.P. worked three evenings a week and all day Saturday. Yet he kept his grades up. He knew that his parents worried about him but he assured them that he was doing well. Upon graduation he earned a full scholarship to the University of Illinois.

By this time Oskar, J.P.'s father was well enough to work from home on the computer as a customer service rep. He also began working with wood making furniture for young children.

When J.P. reached his senior year of college he met Glen at a fraternity party. During their conversation they found out they both enjoyed all types of biking. That was the beginning of their friendship.

The summer before their senior year begun Glen invited J.P. to his home. Glen's parents wanted to talk with J.P. again. Usually Glen's family traveled but had decided to open their home in Aspen Colorado. J.P., with his parent's okay, was going to spend a month in Colorado.

That experience fortified his dreams of wealth. The house was magnificent. It wasn't the largest but from J.P. point of view it was awesome. It had 5 bedrooms, 7 bathrooms, an open kitchen with the dining table seating for 8. J.P. couldn't stop gushing about not only the beautiful home but the view of the mountains was breathtaking.

"This is what I've wanted all my life." J.P. said to Glen once they were in the bedroom that they would share.

"Yeah, I really like this house. But for me, I like something not so flashy." Glen said. He then went on to explain that his parents and older brother were all about money, and social position. However he, his sister and his other brother appreciated what they did but each wanted to do more to help the less fortunate.

J.P. wasn't in agreement with his friend. And he couldn't wait to meet other residents of this area. And Glen didn't fail in that. Glen introduced J.P to some of his friends that were addicted to mountain biking. It didn't take long for J.P to get hooked. He loved it. Hiking, camping were activities that he learned to enjoy. That month flew by quickly. But what he experienced in Aspen and the surrounding area made him realize even more that money would give him this lifestyle. And he seemed to crave it all the more.

Glen's father, Bryant, took time to listen to J.P.'s business idea. And was properly impressed. So much so that he encouraged him to put his business proposal in writing, submit it to him. "I want to help young people like you. No one was there for me. However, J.P. I like your demeanor, confidence and I think your idea is solid." They shook hands.

Glen explained that his father's handshake was as good as if they had a written contract. Glen's folks only stayed in Aspen for 3 weeks. They then took off to Fiji. Brian, Glen's brother, left to visit friends in California and Cheryl, Glen's sister, decided to stay. She would be starting a new job in August. The second son left for Europe.

The threesome hiked Smuggler Mountain Road on the first day. The views were great and the mines were interesting to explore. Returning to the house, Glen fixed a meal of spaghetti with a marinara meat sauce, and garlic bread. J.P. made an Italian green salad while Cheryl set the table and uncorked the wine.

"This is great!" J.P. said as they began eating

"Yeah, it was a fantastic hike. But I think I'll rest tomorrow. My knee is bothering me." Cheryl said.

"Sorry to hear that Sis. But since you won't be with us I'll take J.P. to the Ute Trail." Glen said with a grin.

J.P. tilted his head wondering what Glen was up to. Cheryl giggled, shaking her head from side to side.

"Should I be worried?" J.P. asked.

"No, just be prepared. It's about a 5-mile hike. But it is worth the effort. It's a little over 4 hours and I think Glen just wants to challenge your stamina."

The trek was a challenge but as Cheryl said it was worth it. J.P. found it difficult to put into words the vast beauty of the mountains and valleys. This experience of being in Colorado sealed J.P.'s idea that money was the key to everything.

Now, he thought he had it all. That is until a pretty woman joined him on the elevator one morning. His life, his thoughts gradually began to change. Lauren had somehow wormed her way into his psychic. He'd tried to fight the feelings that he was experiencing by going out with gorgeous women. But it didn't help. He found himself eager to see Lauren on those morning elevator rides, and their lunches on Wednesday. And just calling and talking to her in the evenings. She could make him laugh.

Where was she now? Was she seeing someone else?

LAUREN HESS

*L*auren had missed the filing deadline for the bar exam in September but she did file before November 1st and paid the late fee. With the holidays looming she decided to have an extended visit with her grandparents.

She needed a change of scenery. Pops and Betty were going to Hawaii for 3 weeks, Shenell was going to visit her family in Missouri. Jeanette and Chris were going skiing and then New Zealand. "It's summer down there." Chris said.

Lauren had returned to work at 2BFit but she'd schedule time off for herself.

Being with her mother's family always made her happy. And since she'd terminated her relationship with Marcus, she wanted to get away.

As Lauren drove to her grandparent's home she wondered why she had tried to make the relationship with Marcus work. He was kind but she couldn't reconcile her feelings of his attitude toward the races. Whenever they were out and he saw a racially mixed couple he'd make a snide remark. And even though he was cordial toward her father, she could sense his anger.

Maybe she was on the rebound from J.P. and just wanted to have someone to love. Also, when they kissed she didn't feel the sensation that she felt with J.P.

Oh, J.P. why can't I get you out of my mind and my heart? Lauren thought. Even now after all these weeks she still yearned for his touch, his smile and his kiss. Taking her eyes off the road for a second she glanced at her traveling companion. Allan had given her a chocolate cavapoo puppy. He said, "I don't want you to be on the road alone. Besides, you need something to love other than me."

Lauren smiled thinking about that moment. Allan seemed to be trying to make up for the years that he wasn't in her life. She was loving him without all that he'd given her. And she was very happy that he'd found love again with Betty.

It was a very cold January day. As soon as she pulled into the driveway, her grandfather opened the door. He was tall and still agile for a man in his mid-sixties. He got her luggage while she collected the puppy and all the doggie stuff.

Once inside and after the hugs and kisses, she put her things in the guest bedroom. Then she joined Eddie and Violette in the kitchen.

"Yum-m-m. Something smells wonderful." Lauren said.

"I made vegetable beef soup and cornbread." Vi said.

"That sounds perfect."

The kitchen was a galley style with the table and chairs in a corner nook by the windows. Eddie was already at the table having poured steaming hot chocolate into large mugs.

As the threesome sat down, Vi began to ladle the stew into beautiful navy blue and white porcelain bowls. Lauren asked about her uncles and their families.

Eddie, always the proud father, couldn't help but brag about the grandchildren.

"You'll see them this week!" Vi said. "We decided that we haven't all been together in a couple of years. Your uncles want to see you. And so, we're going over to Theo's house this coming Friday." Because he's your oldest uncle."

Lauren was elated with the prospect of seeing her family. After her mother's funeral, family gatherings seemed to stop. Michael had never gotten along with Monica's parents. Therefore, Lauren and her siblings stayed in contact.

Once they were old enough Tamara and Tony would make the effort but Lauren was young. She missed out on many of the family gatherings. In hindsight, Lauren figured Michael felt that he was punishing Monica by not letting Lauren get to know her maternal family.

The week passed by quickly. It had been awhile since Lauren laughed so much. And to feel such familial bonding was a great sensation. One that she knew she'd never forget.

The last day of her visit Vi and Lauren were alone. Eddie had gone on an errand.

Sitting at the kitchen table drinking hot tea, Vi asked a question. "Lauren, I know many young women these days are all about having a career. But you don't even have a boyfriend. Why not?"

"I'm not the type, grammie." Lauren answered with a sigh.

"You've had your heart broken, haven't you."

Lauren looked at her grandmother in surprise. Then she just nodded as she controlled the tears that threatened to flow.

"It's alright. Your mom's friend Shanell contacted us sometime ago. We were happy to learn that Michael wasn't your father. I'm sorry our Monica didn't tell any of us the truth. Thank goodness for Shanell.

So you've met your birth father, right? And how's that going?"

"It's going great! He's the kindest, most patient person I've ever known." Lauren said. Then she began telling Grammie all about Allan. How he's spoiling her by giving gifts in order to make-up for the years he wasn't with her. "I also found out from Shanell that he did attend both my elementary and high school graduations. Shanell was his link to all of my activities."

"Wow!" Vi exclaimed after Lauren paused to take a breath.

Eddie came in just as Lauren finished speaking. "Are you having fun?" Both women smiled and nodded. After another hour Lauren left to head back to Chicago.

Lauren's life was so different now. She really hadn't answered her grandmother's question about a broken heart but Lauren felt that she hadn't quite gotten over J.P. But she also knew that it would take time. The pain was getting less.

And when Jeanette heard about a sublet in her building she'd contacted Lauren. So Lauren was moving into her own place. With the money from the trust and her inheritance, and by being wise with her spending she would be alright financially. And she was going to return to 2 BFit. Derek still wanted her as the front desk coordinator.

JEANETTE AND CHRIS' WEDDING

"I want a small wedding but Chris is leaning toward a large wedding.

Lauren, what do you think?" Jeanette asked.

The two friends were sitting in Lauren's newly furnished apartment.

"Why are you asking me? What does your mother suggest?"

"My mother doesn't care. She just says that she wants me to be happy. That's what she has always said most of my life. That's how I got pregnant in my teens."

"Jeanette, you've never told me this!" Lauren said as she reached out with her hand to squeeze her friend's hand.

"Yes, I know. I've tried to keep it a secret but I need to have a clean conscience. I just told Chris the other day. And you know what he said?" Jeanette choked up before speaking. Lauren didn't speak but waited.

"He said that he loved me. When we get pregnant, he will spoil me all the more. Then we kissed. I cried. He just held me. I guess I'd been holding that in since I was 15."

Lauren hugged her friend and they both sobbed. After a few minutes, they wiped their eyes and blew their noses. "I think we need a glass of wine." Lauren said before standing up. As she walked into the kitchen Lauren thought about Jeanette's reveal. They had known each other for over 8 years and this is the first time Jeanette had shared this information. Obviously, Chris and the prospect of marriage was going to be a good for her.

Returning to the living room with two glasses and the wine bottle Lauren sat down. Her puppy Cocoa joined her making himself comfortable by Lauren's hip.

"Your puppy is so cute." Jeanette said.

"Yes, and he knows it. But he gets me up in the mornings. We walk for about half an hour at least 3–4 times a week." Lauren said as she stroked the pup's head.

"That's great."

Lauren poured the wine and they began talking about the plans for the wedding. Lauren was surprised when Jeannette said that J.P. offered the use of the hospitality rooms on the top floor of his condo building.

"Why would he do that?"

"Well, since he hired Chris they've become really good friends. I've even met Glen and his wife Jackie. And this will surprise you but I've even gone bike riding with them." Jeanette announced.

"And why am I just now hearing about this?" Lauren asked in an annoyed voice.

"Honestly, I didn't quite know how to tell you. Remember you kind of lost it when you discovered who J.P. was. I was put in a weird position. He was contacting me and you weren't. Then you were dating Marcus. You wouldn't mention J.P. so I kept quiet." Jeanette said before picking up her wine glass to take a sip.

Lauren sighed as she leaned back on the couch cushions. She had been acting weird. But now her focus was different. She'd be taking the bar exam soon and her father was already talking to people about hiring her. J.P. was the past.

And she had to admit that she'd forbid Jeanette to mention his name. She now realized that it was her fear of loss and anger of being decieved. Her mother, Michael and then J.P., these were people she'd loved and each had in their own way not been 100% honest. But why was J.P. the hardest one to forgive?

"Hey, Lauren, are you with me?" Jeanette asked.

"Oh, yes sorry. I just got lost in thought. So let's get back to the important stuff. You're renting your bridal gown, right? And Louise and I are your bridesmaids."

"Yes. but you are the maid-of-honor. And I have the perfect dresses for each of you!" Jeanette smiled.

"So next week we'll have the fittings. May will be here before you know it." Jeanette said.

The second Saturday in May at 3:00 in the afternoon everything was ready. The wedding ceremony was to be at Navy Pier with just family and close friends in attendance. It was a breezy afternoon with the waves of Lake Michigan splashing over the pier wall.

As Lauren walked down the aisle she focused forward. She knew that J.P was sitting with the guests but she feared her reaction if she saw him. It had been about 8 months since they'd been together. And yet, no matter how hard she tried he was a fixture in her heart. Once she was in her place in front, she watched Jeanette coming down the aisle. The attendance on Jeanette's side consisted of her mother, some cousins, former co-workers and current co-workers.

Chris beamed as he watched his love approaching him. His large family included his parents, 5 uncles with wives and children. His two brothers were standing with him as his ushers.

Jeanette's lilac dress complimented her blonde tip braid and dark eyes. While Louise's dress was amethyst, Lauren's dress was heliotrope. Each carried a small bouquet of white roses with Jeanette's bouquet having a mix of lilac and purple flowers.

While the nuptials were being said Lauren allowed herself to look at the audience. There, standing on Jeanette's family side behind the chairs was J.P. His gaze was fixed on her and he smiled when he caught her eye. Lauren quickly returned her eyes back to Chris and Jeanette. Her heart was racing and her breath was shallow. *I've got control,* Lauren said to herself.

J.P.'s condo building was only about 3 blocks away. After the photographs were taken of the bridal party, family and friends all made their way to the reception.

The top floor of the building gave a panoramic view of the lake and the north shore. The open bar and the buffet was ready and waiting for the wedding attendees and those who were invited to attend the reception only.

Music, dancing and laughter filled the room. J.P. circled the room like a predator waits and watches his prey. He continued to keep his distance from Lauren without taking his eyes off of her. She did her best to ignore him but to no avail. She did her maid of honor duties and danced with different men. But it wasn't until Dereck had her on the dance floor.

"Lauren, you look exceptionally lovely." Dereck said as he pulled her close.

"Dereck, please you're holding me too tight." Lauren said as she attempted to put some light between them.

"Lauren, you know how I've felt about you. Why don't you…"

Before Dereck finished his sentence, J.P. tapped him on the shoulder. "May I cut in?" J.P.'s voice was authoritative as he looked into Dereck's eyes.

Dereck looked from J.P. back to Lauren. Then he said, "Sure, if the lady wishes."

Like a moth to a flame Lauren seemed to float into J.P.'s arms. J.P. nodded in the direction of the dj. And the song "You Make Me Smile by Brian Culbertson" filled the room.

It was too perfect.

"I've missed this." J.P. said softly. "Lauren please can you forgive me for not being completely honest with you?"

Lauren didn't speak immediately. She was just happy being where she belonged, in J.P.'s arms.

"Yes, I forgave you a while ago. But my fear stopped me."

"I promise that I'll not deceive you again. It was just that you messed up my schedule. I wasn't suppose to meet and fall in love until I was 40."

"Oh really. Well, I guess we'll have to wait. But I'm not promising that I'll be available at that time." Lauren teased.

J.P. laughed. "I've missed you so much." Taking her by the hand he led her off the dance floor. Finding a quiet corner, he kissed her.

"We need to talk." he said as they walked toward the elevator. Holding her close around her waist, he asked, "Will you marry me?" He pushed the elevator button.

"But I'm not pretty like the women I'm sure you've been with." Lauren said as she looked into his eyes.

"No, you're not pretty. You're beautiful and I'm so in love with you. My life was empty until last summer when we met." J.P. said.

"Yes, I'll marry you!" Lauren said with a giggle.

The elevator doors opened and they stepped inside.

"Where are we going?" Lauren asked.

"To my place and to Las Vegas." J.P. said. As the elevator doors began closing.

"But why?"

"Because you said yes."

Their beginning!